Enter at Your Own Risk

by R. A. Noonan

ALADDIN PAPERBACKS

Copyright © 1995 by Twelfth House Productions

Aladdin Paperbacks
An imprint of Simon & Schuster
Children's Publishing Division
1230 Avenue of the Americas
New York, NY 10020

First Aladdin Paperbacks edition September 1995

Manufactured in the United States of America

10 9 8 7 6 5 4 3 2 1

Library of Congress Cataloging-in-Publication Data

Noonan, R. A.
Enter at your own risk / by R. A. Noonan. — 1st
Aladdin Paperbacks ed.
p.   cm. — (Monsterville ; #1)
Summary: After running away from home, ten-year-old
Darcy and her cousins Sam and Fiona stumble into a
cave inhabited by a variety of monsters who think
humans are nothing but trouble.
ISBN 0-689-71863-2
[1. Monsters—Fiction. 2. Runaways—Fiction.
3. Caves—Fiction.] I. Title. II. Series: Noonan, R. A.
Monsterville ; #1.
PZ7.N753En 1995
[Fic]—dc20   95-3173

In memory of Frances Turnley,
a fairy godmother who
understood wishes and magic dust

Prologue

The steady beat of the black bat's wings cut through the air over Main Street. No one in Whiterock, Montana, noticed the creature soaring against the blue sky. No one knew they were being watched as the bat circled on a wind current.

Not the man climbing out of the black Jeep. Not the woman pushing her stroller with a young one inside. Not the man whittling a piece of wood in front of the feed store.

The bat let out a squeak, but no one heard.

They don't even know I'm here, thought Draku. *But I see them. I see that they're getting close . . . too close. It's time to warn the others. Sound the alarm. Save ourselves before the humans come!*

He pumped his muscles and his rubbery wings flapped again, lifting him high over the old western town. The crowned rooftops sped beneath him. Then came the square roof of the middle school, and the blacktopped playground dotted with children.

The noise here was so disturbing. It made his

1

large, pointed ears twitch with pain.

Young, shrill voices. So high-pitched! Their shouts threw his sonar off.

Children! How did the humans tolerate them?

Beating his wings faster, he soared ahead. Hayfields and green meadows crisscrossed the ground like a patchwork quilt. He raced over the crazy pattern, heading toward the border—the purple mountains on the horizon.

The Bitterroot Range.

These lumbering mountains had been a good home for many years. Quiet. Secluded. Uninhabited.

But that was changing quickly.

The humans were ruining the place. Laughing in the sunlight. Shouting into the breeze. Chattering twenty-four hours a day. Sheesh! It was enough to drive anyone batty.

At the edge of the range, the bat flew over a dirt road that curved around the side of one mountain. The steep hillside was covered with tall weeds, over-grown vines, and trees. But he knew the way in.

Diving in between the three tall pine trees, he pressed into the shadows and entered the mouth of the cave.

Tha-thump . . . tha-thump . . . His flapping wings echoed through the cool, dark passage. Navigating carefully, he moved through the tunnel. After what he'd seen out there, it would be good to get home.

At last he reached the back wall of the cave. Hovering patiently, he waited for the vision to come.

It always happened slowly . . . mysteriously. The brown rock wall began to swirl, like a smoky dream. Then it faded into dust. . . .

And finally the entrance appeared.

Like a door to a magic land, the arched opening glowed. Draku felt warmed by luminescence. The walls glittered with diamond-etched crystals. The tinkling sound of an icicle wind chime filled the passage—a welcoming sound to the bat's tired ears.

Ahh, sweet home. Not even a skeptic like Draku could deny it. This place was truly enchanted.

And it will stay that way, he thought, *as long as we keep those miserable humans out!*

1

Ms. Blundell's English class was always the low point of Darcy Ryan's day. A jumble of nerves, Darcy sat at her desk and stared down at the open book. Black letters swam and bounced along the white page, taunting her.

Read us! Read us! But first, you've got to catch us!

Why couldn't she focus?

And soon it would be her turn. Two seats away, Mary Ann Hargrove was reading aloud. Jay Greenberg would be next. Then Darcy. She was doomed! Her life was over, finished . . . history.

She twirled one of her gold braids around her finger. Mary Ann sounded so convincing. The words floated from her lips. How did she turn all the squiggles on the page into a story?

"Very good, Mary Ann," Ms. Blundell said. She nodded at Jay. "You can start with the next paragraph."

"I am the ghost of Jacob Marley!" Jay growled dramatically.

Kids snickered. Jay Greenberg turned every assignment into a goofy show. But this time, Darcy couldn't laugh. She was too nervous about going next.

"All right, Jay," Ms. Blundell said a few moments later. "Next?" Her eyes flickered to Darcy with an encouraging look that said, *Go ahead.*

Steeling her nerves, Darcy took a deep breath. . . .

And then the bell rang.

Yes!

"We'll pick up with you tomorrow, Darcy," Ms. Blundell said, closing her book. "Don't forget your homework assignment, class. Chapter five of . . ."

Darcy tuned out the rest. *I'll have to go first*, she thought. In a cloud of gloom, she stacked her books and headed out into the hall. She couldn't read aloud. She'd have to stay home sick tomorrow.

And for the rest of her life.

Darcy couldn't stand the embarrassment of failing in front of the other kids in her class. Since second grade, she'd managed to get by with the help of her best friend, Kate Capezio. Every night they'd met to do their homework together, and Kate had coached her along. They'd studied for tests together. If there was a group project, they were partners.

But now Kate was gone. Over the summer the Capezios had moved to Idaho, where Kate's dad got a job. Just like that, Darcy had lost her best friend! She really missed Kate. And since school had started last month, Darcy had realized how much Kate had helped her with homework.

Without Kate, she was going to flunk.

Darcy couldn't keep up with her assignments. She'd already failed two tests. Whenever she was called on in class she had to fish for an answer— either make one up or beg off with some excuse.

So far she'd gotten away with a few curious looks from other kids. But her luck was running out. Mid-term warning letters had already been sent out to parents, and Darcy had a feeling that her name was on the black list. That would send Mom through the roof!

And tomorrow, when Ms. Blundell made her read aloud in class, everyone would discover her secret . . . that she wasn't very smart at all. In fact, if you looked at her grades, you'd think she was stupid.

But grades aren't everything, Darcy reminded herself. When she worked on her mother's ranch, Darcy felt very smart. She was a terrific trick rider. She taught little kids how to treat the animals. And there wasn't a horse in the world she couldn't win over.

Too bad ranching skills didn't account for much in school.

Darcy was so caught up in her problems she didn't notice Nora Chambers calling her . . . until Nora yanked on her sleeve.

"Earth to Darcy," Nora said. Her braces twinkled as she grinned. "We're going into town. Want to come? Milk shakes from the Dairy Saloon."

Behind Nora, Brook Lauer nodded shyly, her orange ponytail bobbing. "Come with us."

"No, thanks," Darcy said reluctantly. She slammed her locker door. "I gotta get home."

"Aw, come on," Nora wheedled. "You never hang around with us after school. Is it the—"

"I really gotta go," Darcy interrupted. "We have a new foal on the ranch and my mom needs help taking care of her." It was sort of a lie. Gingersnap was already three weeks old. But what was she supposed to say? *I've got to get home and snag the midsemester warning letter before my mom sees it. You see, I'm failing English. Flunking out.*

Unfortunately, the lie backfired.

"A baby horse?" Nora blinked in surprise. "Way cool. What's its name? Did you watch it get born?"

Brook's eyes grew wide with awe. "Can we see it?"

"Sure, um"—Darcy stuttered—"maybe next week." She hitched her knapsack up on her shoulder and backed down the hall. "She's still a little shy right now. Well . . . see you tomorrow."

Afraid that someone else would snag her, Darcy moved like the wind. She darted between kids in the crowded corridor. Outside, she raced to the bicycle stand and hopped on her ten-speed.

Her bike seemed to know the way down the shady streets swarming with kids. She rolled past the neat rows of houses. Then there were fields of swaying hay. The Ryan ranch was on the outskirts of town, just a fifteen-minute bike ride from school.

The wind tossed wisps of blond hair away from her face as Darcy stared ahead. *Maybe the letter won't be there. Maybe I'm doing better than I thought.*

But there was no use fooling herself. Darcy knew she had a problem at school. And it made her sick to her stomach. Every night, she went to the window and picked out her lucky star. It was the first one to light the sky, blinking green through the branches of the big oak tree. "Please, make me smart!" she'd call out.

So far, her wish hadn't come true.

She spotted the cluster of mailboxes up the road. Pumping harder and harder, she brought the bike up to racer speed. *Here goes,* she thought, soaring ahead.

The red flags were pointed up. The mail carrier had been here. Darcy swerved to a stop and opened the door of the white box marked Ryan.

There was a glossy magazine . . . and a bunch of envelopes. She leafed through them—mostly bills—until the crisp envelope came to the top. The return address was printed in the corner in stern black letters: Whiterock Elementary School.

This was definitely it—her letter of doom.

Pressing the stack of mail to her chest, she tore it open and studied the swimming print. She couldn't decipher the whole thing. But the word "failure" jumped out at her. She sounded out one line.

"Back to the fourth grade."

The fourth grade! Darcy's eyes began to burn with tears. Wasn't flunking bad enough? They wanted to yank her away from her friends and toss her in with the fourth graders!

2

Sam Mackie pushed the visor of his Chicago Cubs hat up and eyed the crowd of kids outside the Dairy Saloon. The ice-cream parlor was a popular hangout. But Sam liked to imagine what had happened at the saloon years ago, when gunslingers and gold miners ruled.

No parents. No hyper little sisters. No country kids who resent you because you used to live in a big city.

Just the road west . . . and a faithful horse.

Horse? Who am I kidding? If my cousin Darcy weren't so patient, I'd still be trying to figure out how to stay in the saddle.

Riding was just one of the things Sam had taken on since the move. "You'll love the great outdoors," Dad kept saying.

Yeah? When? Sam wanted to ask.

Life in Chicago had been better. You could hit the aquarium, catch a movie, *and* see a baseball game in one afternoon.

Out here, you had to have a satellite dish just to get the local news.

I'd go back to the city in a second, Sam thought as he climbed onto the wooden boardwalk in front of the row of shops. Down at the end of the block, beside Silverado Realty, was his father's office, with its sign carved in gold letters: CHARLES MACKIE, ATTORNEY-AT-LAW. Sam tugged open the door and ducked inside.

The office was a homey old shop filled with gently worn furniture and braided rugs. His father's office was separated by a glass panel, and Sam could hear his dad talking to someone inside.

"Hi, Agnes." Sam grinned at the woman manning the reception desk. A member of the Blackfeet Indian nation, Agnes had warm brown skin and shiny dark eyes.

"Hey, Sam," she greeted him, staring at Sam over her spectacles.

Sam was supposed to pick up his sister, Fiona, but he didn't see her in the waiting area. "Where's Fee?"

"I guess her bus is late again," said Agnes.

"Again," Sam repeated. It was like this every day. Although the grade school got out a half hour earlier than Sam's school, the bus trip always made his sister late. "I can't wait until Fiona is old enough to take care of herself."

Agnes frowned behind her glasses. "Baby-sitting blues?"

"I've got my own stuff to do," Sam complained. He edged toward his dad's office, where the men's voices were still rumbling. The doorway was wide open, and Sam poked his head inside.

From behind his desk, Charles Mackie caught Sam's eye and shook his head abruptly. Whatever the men were discussing, Sam could tell that it made his father uncomfortable.

Scooting out of the doorway, Sam went to the glass panel separating the waiting area from his father's office. If he lifted a corner of the blinds, he could see inside.

"I recently bought a plot of land near here," the client said. He was a large man with a square jaw and wide shoulders. Sunglasses covered his eyes, and the way he sat, so stiff and straight, reminded Sam of a soldier. The man reached for a cardboard tube and unrolled a map on the desk. "I need some special permits, and the town clerk said you could draw up the paperwork. This is the parcel."

Sam's father glanced down at the map. "Hidden Canyon?" He blinked in surprise.

The man nodded. "That's it."

"Do you know the drawbacks of the area?" Mr. Mackie asked. "The fog never lifts from that valley. It's ringed by mountains, and there's no way in. No one's seen the canyon since an avalanche wiped out the access road in the eighteen hundreds."

Sam's father had grown up in Whiterock and

knew all kinds of things about the area. But the client didn't seem to care.

"I've surveyed the area," the man said. "That parcel suits my needs. All I need to do is build an access road. That's why I need the permits."

Curious, Sam pressed closer to the glass. Who was this guy?

Charles Mackie leaned back in his chair. "What kind of paperwork are we talking about?"

"Blasting permits," the stranger said. "I'm going to blow a hole in the mountains around that canyon. A few sticks of dynamite should do it."

Dynamite! The hair on the back of Sam's neck tingled.

Mr. Mackie scratched his chin the way he always did when he was stalling for time. Sam could tell that his father wasn't too happy about this guy's plan.

"That's an expensive proposition," Sam's father said. "Mind if I ask what you plan to do with the land once you blast your way in?"

The man was cold as a stone wall. "I really couldn't say. But I'd like to get the paperwork going." He reached into the pocket of his leather jacket, pulled out a card, and started writing on the back. "Give me a call at the Deer Leap Inn when you've got the permits ready. Here's the number."

Taking the business card, Charles Mackie glanced at the number. "Mr. Pride, I'm afraid I don't feel right about getting involved without more information."

"I'll make it worth your while," the man said.

Sam was waiting for his father's answer when Fiona blew in the door. The hood of her pink windbreaker was pulled over her dark curls, even though it wasn't cold outside.

"Hi, Agnes!" she chirped, dancing in. "I'm a butterfly in our class play. Ms. Vandermeer wants me to practice being graceful." She flapped her arms and knocked a magazine off the coffee table.

"Easy, squirt," Sam warned.

Fiona blinked at him. "What's going on?" Before anyone could answer, she was climbing onto the chair beside Sam, rattling the blinds. "Who's that?"

"Shh," Sam whispered. "Dad's in a meeting with an important client."

"An important giant?"

"*Cli-ent*," Sam said carefully.

"Oh." Annoyed, Fiona tugged on the shades. They crackled under her fingers, then smacked against the glass, causing both men to look over.

"I'll be with you kids in a minute," Mr. Mackie called out. The warning tone of his voice said: Pipe down out there.

"Real subtle, Fee," Sam muttered under his breath.

"Thanks," she said cheerfully.

Sam sank down into a chair. Fiona was such a pest. Were all six-year-olds nosy fidgets?

Although Sam couldn't see inside the office, he

could still hear their voices through the open door.

"Without more information, I can't help you," Sam's father said.

"This is a multimillion-dollar deal," the man said. "And I just might be willing to give you a cut."

Millions? Dollar bills danced before Sam's eyes as he listened for his father's answer.

"Not interested," Mr. Mackie said firmly. "And it's only fair to warn you that the people in this town won't approve the sale unless you present plans. We have zoning laws. Environmental regulations . . ."

"Hogwash," the big man growled. "I didn't come here for approval. And there's no one in this one-horse town with the power to stop me."

Sam backed away from the open doorway as the man strode out. He looked overpowering—like an irate bear. Through the shop window, Sam watched him climb into a black Jeep and pull away.

Fiona wrinkled her nose. "He's a grump."

But Sam was already in his father's office. "You really toasted that guy's waffles, Dad."

Mr. Mackie smiled. "That wasn't my intention."

"What do you think he's planning to do with Hidden Canyon?"

"Who knows?" His father raked back his dark curls and sighed. "I'd better make a few calls about Mr. Marshall Pride. The guy looks like an ex-military man. Maybe one of my army buddies knows him."

Wishing he could be involved, Sam ran his hands over the edge of his father's desk. This was the most exciting thing that had happened since they'd moved to Whiterock. "Anything you want me to do?" he volunteered. "I could ask around. Maybe look up his name on the reference computer at the library."

"Oh, let me do that," Fiona said. "Ms. Vandermeer taught us to use it. And I can spell Pride. P-R-I—"

"Thanks for the offer." Charles Mackie came out from behind his desk. "But I think I can handle this." He ruffled Fiona's curly brown bangs as he walked the kids to the door. "You guys better get home and dig into that schoolwork."

Typical, Sam thought. *Instead of helping Dad investigate, I get stuck baby-sitting.*

"Come on," he said, tugging on Fiona's hood.

Another exciting afternoon with a six-year-old.

3

Marshall Pride's image was still burning in Sam's brain as he walked home. The dark glasses. The heavy boots. The broad shoulders. Pride reminded Sam of a cartoon villain who threatened to take over the world.

Unaffected, Fiona ambled along beside him, singing under her breath. But as soon as they turned onto their block, she stopped abruptly. Her dark eyes squinted toward their house. Then a smile broke out on her face. "Darcy!" she called, racing ahead.

Sam was surprised to see his cousin. She usually spent her afternoons with friends from school. From the way she was hunkered down on the porch steps, her chin in her hands, he could tell she was in a glum mood.

When the Mackies first moved to Whiterock, Sam and Fiona barely knew Darcy. They had only met a few times during vacations. But over the past few weeks, Sam had gotten to know Darcy better.

The cousin thing was okay—sort of like having a sister who didn't get on your nerves.

"Hey, Darce," he said.

"Hay is for horses," Darcy muttered.

Fiona crouched down and peered into Darcy's face. "Are you having a bad day?"

"That's for sure." Darcy's blue eyes were stormy as she glanced up at Sam. "I'm in trouble."

His mouth dropped open in surprise. "You? You never get in trouble. You're a total perfectionist."

"But I'm not so good at school," Darcy said sadly. She reached into her denim jacket and pulled out a white envelope. "See?"

Sam read the letter quickly. It was a note to Darcy's mother from the vice principal at Whiterock Elementary School. He wanted to have a meeting about Darcy's "poor performance." It even mentioned pushing her back to the fourth grade.

Fiona sat down on the porch and leaned against Darcy. "What's it say?"

Sam frowned. "Just that Darcy is . . . having some problems at school," he told his little sister. He didn't mention the part about demoting her.

"Oh." Fiona pressed her fingers against her lips thoughtfully. "That's not so bad." She turned to Darcy. "Want to hear my lines for the class play?"

"Maybe later," Darcy said. "Right now I've got to figure out what to do next."

"What *can* you do?" Sam asked. "Let your mother go to the meeting and see what they can work out. I mean, how bad could it be?"

"I could be the moron of the fourth grade," Darcy pointed out shakily. "Everybody'll know I was pushed back a grade. I'll be marked as a loser forever."

Sam tucked the letter back into the envelope. "Have you ever gotten a letter like this before?"

Darcy shook her head. "I've never been great in school, but I always had my friend Kate to help me out." She explained how she and Kate used to work together. "But Kate's family just moved to a town on the other side of the Bitterroots. Over in Idaho."

"I hate moving," Fiona announced.

"Well, maybe you can find a tutor who'll help you the way Kate did," Sam suggested.

But a new wave of tears filled Darcy's eyes. "I'm doomed! My mom and dad have a deal. As long as I do okay in school, I can stay on the ranch. But Dad's always wanted me to live with him in Seattle. He says the schools are better there, and now my mom will have to send me to live with him. Not that it'll matter to her. She's so busy with the ranch, she'll hardly notice that I'm gone." She squeezed her eyes tight to hold back the tears.

"Aw, Darcy . . ." Sam wasn't sure what to say.

Darcy's parents had split up when she was five. Every summer she spent two weeks with her father in Seattle. Darcy and her dad got along fine. But

Sam couldn't imagine Darcy leaving the Ryan ranch forever.

Fiona squeezed Darcy's arm. "I don't want you to go away."

"I don't want to go," Darcy sobbed.

"Come on inside, you guys," Sam said. "We'll figure out something."

An hour later, Sam scrolled through the page on his monitor. "How would she sign it?" he asked Darcy, who was sitting cross-legged on his bed. "Mrs. P. Ryan? Or just Ms. Pamela Ryan?"

Darcy ran her hand over the pattern on the comforter as she considered the question. "Probably just Pam Ryan. She's not big on formal stuff."

Sam typed in the last few words, then popped the disk out of his computer. "Perfecto. Now we just print out a copy on Dad's computer and we're in."

With a hopeful smile, Darcy followed him down the hall to the den. As they passed the family room, Fiona looked up from the table.

"Come see my butterfly wings!" she ordered. She'd spent the last half hour working on her costume for the class play. "They've got glitter and dots."

"In a minute, squirt," Sam called. Inside the den, he switched on his father's computer, popped in the disk, then hit the keys to print.

The letter to the vice-principal was just the first part of their plan. Trying to sound like Aunt Pam, Sam had drafted a note explaining that Darcy hadn't been feeling well, but would work even harder in the weeks ahead.

The letter was pretty convincing, even if Sam did feel guilty about writing it. After all, it was a lie.

But if it would keep Darcy here in Whiterock, it was worth twisting the truth. As far as Sam was concerned, his cousin was one of the few good things about living in Dullsville, USA. Besides, he couldn't stand to see her cry.

Part two of the plan: cousin Sam. He was going to tutor Darcy. If a ten-year-old girl could do it, why couldn't Sam?

The white sheet of paper rolled out of the printer, and Sam picked it up and read it aloud.

Darcy listened, biting her lips nervously. When Sam finished, she asked, "Do you think it'll work?"

"No question," Sam said, handing her the letter. "Problem solved. I say we've earned a serious snack."

"Got any cookies?" Darcy asked.

Sam grinned. "Double fudge."

"Last one in the kitchen eats carrot sticks," Darcy said, racing down the hall. She beat Sam to the kitchen, where she carefully placed the note on the clean part of the counter, next to the dreaded letter that had started all her troubles.

Sam was stacking cookies, crackers, milk, and

juice on the table when Fiona shouted from the family room.

"Sam! I spilled the glitter. And it got onto Dad's chair . . . ox-identally."

"Aw, man," Sam muttered as he and Darcy flew down the hall. That worn-out chair was one of his father's favorite things in the world. If anything happened to it, Sam would be grounded for a hundred years.

When he reached the den door, Sam's mouth dropped open.

It was worse than he'd expected.

Fiona beat at a cushion, making the shiny specks jump into the air. She glanced up with a guilty smile.

"How did you spill a whole jar?" Darcy asked. "And down into the seams . . ."

Fiona shrugged. "I don't know."

"That's it with the glitter," Sam said sternly. "Never again."

Fiona's lower lip stuck out in a pout. But for once she had the sense to keep quiet.

"Now get the broom and dustpan," he ordered.

Sam manned the vacuum, while Darcy and Fiona wiped up glue and paint.

The noise of the vacuum was so loud, Sam didn't hear his mother come in. Lila Mackie was usually in a good mood when she got home from her job at the library. But as soon as she appeared in the doorway of the family room, Sam could tell something was wrong.

Her eyes burned with anger as she stood there holding up two pieces of white paper—the letters. She must have seen them on the kitchen counter, where Darcy had left them.

Sam switched off the vacuum and stood up. Behind him, Darcy was dead silent.

"Hi, Mom," Fiona chirped. "Want to see my wings? I'm the butterfly in the—"

"In a few minutes, dear," Mrs. Mackie said, not even looking over at Fiona. Under her scowl, Sam felt like a bug pinned down to a board. "Right now I have a few questions for Darcy . . . and your brother. Who's taken up *creative* writing."

Sam and Darcy were busted!

4

By the time Darcy turned down the dirt driveway toward the ranch, it was almost dark. The sun had sunk below the mountains, but a crisp orange light lingered over the jagged peaks.

Her throat was tight as she walked her bike into the mudroom and crept into the kitchen. She expected her mother to be waiting, a look of disappointment on her face.

But the house was empty.

On the kitchen table was a note from Mom.

"Taking a group on a sunset tour. Back before bedtime. Cold chicken and salad in the fridge."

It's just me and the empty house again. For a second, Darcy felt sorry for herself. Her mother spent so much time working the ranch, sometimes Darcy felt as if she lived alone. "I'm going to hire a ranch hand, just as soon as I catch up on these bills," her mother always promised. But it didn't look like things were going to change anytime soon.

Darcy tried to help out. She made her bed and

washed the dishes. She'd learned to cook spaghetti and soup and toasted cheese sandwiches. But it was no fun eating alone, which happened a lot since Mom had tons of chores in the barn at the end of the day.

Her thoughts churning, Darcy paced through the kitchen. On the counter, the answering machine was flashing. Probably a message from Aunt Lila about the terrible things she and Sam had done. *Too bad I had to drag Sam into this mess with me*, Darcy thought.

So . . . Mom didn't know about the trouble yet. Maybe it was a good thing that Mom was so busy. It gave Darcy a chance to save herself . . . but how?

It was time for something really drastic.

Hugging herself, Darcy realized what she had to do. It wouldn't be easy. And the hardest part would be leaving Whiterock . . . the ranch, her cousins, and all the horses.

But what choice did she have? She couldn't stay here and let everyone find out that she was stupid. *Besides*, she reasoned, *Mom will be relieved to have one less person to take care of. Then she can really concentrate on the horses.*

Once the decision was made, Darcy felt better.

Working fast, she erased the messages on the machine. She wrote out a note to her mother, saying that she was spending the night with her cousins. She loaded up her knapsack with all the money from her secret hiding place under a loose floorboard. She grabbed a flashlight and a sleeping bag. Then she threw in snacks from the refrigerator.

There was just one more thing. . . .

She picked up the phone and pecked out the Mackies' number. Lucky for her, Sam answered.

"I just wanted to say good-bye," Darcy told him. "And I'm sorry I got you into trouble."

"Good-bye?" Sam was confused at first. Then, when Darcy explained her plan, he blew up.

"Don't do it! It's too dangerous, Darcy. Or at least wait till the morning. You don't know what—"

"I have to go now," she said, cutting him off. She had to get going before her mom got back. Besides, Sam would keep trying to change her mind. "Tell Fiona I said good-bye, but not until tomorrow." Darcy knew Fiona couldn't keep a secret.

Before Sam could say another word, she hung up and headed out to the barn to say good-bye to the horses.

She had an extra-long hug for Gingersnap. "I wish I could take you with me," she said, brushing her fingers over the filly's velvety neck. But right now Gingersnap needed to stay with her mother. "I love you," Darcy whispered, pressing against the filly one last time.

As she crept out of the barn, Gingersnap let out a curious whinny. But Darcy didn't look back.

She clicked on her flashlight and kept it pointed on the trail that led to the Bitterroots. *I need to get to the foot of the mountains tonight*, she thought. Tomorrow, after the sun came up, she'd walk the rest of the way to Big Moose, where the general store was also a bus depot. Then she could catch the bus to Idaho and begin her new life with Kate's family.

The Capezios had five kids, but Darcy knew they wouldn't mind having her around. Before they left Whiterock, Darcy had spent all her time with the big, noisy family. Every afternoon. Dinner four nights a week. Sleep-overs on weekends. She had fit in so well, sometimes she'd daydreamed about changing her last name to Capezio.

Maybe I'll do that when I reach Idaho, she thought. If Kate's parents didn't mind, Darcy would join their family. Kate could tutor her each day. And Darcy would gladly help out with dishes and the little kids' bathtime.

Then I won't flunk fifth grade, she thought, kicking at the dust along the trail. *And I won't be alone in an empty house, waiting for Mom to come home.*

Life in Idaho was going to be great.

🦇 🦇 🦇

Fiona swung her legs under the dining room table as she chased a spiral of macaroni around her plate. Mac and cheese was her favorite dinner. Too bad Sam had been sent to his room with a sandwich and milk.

"Does Sam get dessert?" she asked her mother.

"Not tonight. And don't swing your legs, honey. It's not polite."

Fiona linked her ankles together and chewed. Funny how she'd spilled the glitter, but Sam had gotten grounded. It was because of some letter he and Darcy had printed up.

Everyone was in a bad mood. Mom was mad at Sam. And Dad was upset about the big man who'd been in his office—Mr. Pride.

"George Mattern knew him in the service," Dad was saying. "He says Pride is a munitions expert."

"I can't believe it," Mom said. "What would a munitions expert want with Hidden Canyon?"

"Nothing good," Dad muttered. "George says Pride has a government contract. He wants to turn the canyon into a munitions dump."

Mom swallowed hard. "How awful! He'll ruin the land."

"What's a you-nishens?" Fiona asked.

"Munitions," Mom repeated. "Weapons. Bombs and guns. Eat your carrots."

"Myou-nishens," Fiona repeated, stabbing a carrot with her fork. Sam would want to know about this.

As soon as Fiona finished eating, she excused herself, put her plate in the sink, and ran upstairs to Sam's room.

"Sam?" She peeked into the dark room, then remembered she was supposed to knock. "Oops!" She tapped on the door as she closed it behind her.

"Knock knock. Guess who?" she said cheerfully. Sam was a lump in the bed, and it wasn't even dessert time yet! "Wake up, sleepyhead. I've got news. And I didn't even have to spy to get it."

She shook his shoulder. It felt mushy under the blanket. "Sam?" She lifted the comforter from his head. . . .

And gasped.

A bunch of pillows were lined up where Sam was supposed to be.

He was gone!

5

The lonely howl shot through the woods.

Coyotes. Darcy paused to button up her denim jacket. She listened carefully, trying to figure out how close the animals were. Their howls seemed to come from far away, but as she'd walked along the trail she'd heard noises behind her. Snapping twigs. Rustling grass.

Were they following her?

Stay cool. Don't panic. She knew that coyotes weren't picky eaters. When it came to survival, they'd attack animals as large as young cattle and deer.

They're probably just as afraid of me as I am of them, Darcy told herself, marching on. Still, she felt a little better when the trail spilled onto the mountain road. There wasn't a car in sight, but the fact that someone could come along made her feel a little safer.

She paused at the roadside and wrapped a yellow twisty-tie around the branch of a tree. For the past two hours she'd been marking her path, just in case something went wrong and she needed to backtrack.

Silence closed in around her. Then she heard the shuffling noises again. They were getting closer.

Thinking fast, she clicked off her flashlight and dived behind a tall clump of prairie grass. Her heartbeat sounded loud in her ears—and she wondered if the approaching creature could smell her fear.

It was coming closer. . . . And closer . . .

Darcy held her breath as the figure broke clear of the woods. It was too tall to be a coyote. Was it a bear?

It climbed onto the roadway, and at last the watery moonlight revealed all.

It was Sam!

Darcy sprang to her feet. "What are *you* doing here?"

Startled, Sam did a quick side step. "I wanted to make sure you got to the bus depot in one piece," he replied.

"Well, I've lived here all my life. I know these mountains like the back of my hand," she insisted.

"Then what's with those yellow things?"

"Just in case," Darcy said, softening. It was sweet of Sam to come after her. "I'm glad you came," she said as they set off down the road. "Are you running away, too?"

Sam didn't know how to answer. He had to go

back home eventually, but right now he wanted to keep his options open. "I'm not sure," he said slowly. "I wouldn't miss much in Whiterock. I mean, it's not like I've made lots of friends since we moved here. Who wants to hang out with a kid who's always baby-sitting?"

"But Fiona's a sweetheart," Darcy said.

"She wears me down. Spying. Reading over my shoulder. Spilling stuff all over the place."

"I know what you mean. Pesky but cute."

"Mostly pesky," Sam declared. "I should probably stay away long enough for my parents to cool down. Mom was fuming about that fake letter. And once they figure out I slipped out of the house, they're going to go ballistic."

"*Your* parents?" Darcy shook her head. "I don't think so. Your mom and dad are the coolest."

🦇 🦇 🦇

Fireworks! Right in her own living room!

Fiona had never seen her parents this mad before. Mom was pacing while Dad heated up like a firecracker with a short fuse. Peering through the rails of the banister, Fiona watched in silence.

She hadn't tipped her parents off about Sam. They'd figured it out when Aunt Pam called to speak to Darcy and found that both of them were gone. Within minutes, the Mackies' living room was the center of the action. Aunt Pam had rushed over. And the sheriff had marched in, his badge sparkling and his heavy boots thudding against the floor.

Sam was *really* in trouble now!

"What in the world are they thinking?" Mom said. "Don't they know it gets cold here after dark?"

"The Bitterroots are dangerous at night," Aunt Pam said. "Darcy knows that. I can't believe she'd do such a foolish thing." She was sitting at the edge of the fireplace, pressing a tissue to her eyes. Aunt Pam was crying!

"We have to go after them," Mom said.

Sheriff Smoke's dark eyes were thoughtful. "Any idea where they might be headed?"

"If I know Sam, he's on a plane back to Chicago," Dad put in, rubbing his eyes. "But he'd have to get to an airport first."

"And Sam knows he'd never make it to the airport on foot," Mom added.

"The mountains," Aunt Pam said. "That's the first place Darcy would go. I think we should follow them on horseback."

"Fine," the sheriff said. "Let's go back to your place and saddle up."

"I'll take the car and check the roads," Dad put in. "We're bound to catch up with them, one way or another. How far could they get on foot?"

"We'll stay in touch by radio," the sheriff said.

Fiona felt a spark of excitement as the adults completed the plans. It was sort of like a scavenger hunt.

With this kind of excitement, the last place she wanted to be was in her boring old bed.

⚫⚫⚫

Ouch, ouch, ouch! With each step, Darcy's feet throbbed inside her boots. But how could she complain? It had been her idea to make this trip.

A towering mountain rose in a wall of rock and trees on their left. To their right the road was lined by forest and weeds. Darcy had been in this area for camping trips. But she'd never hiked so far in one day.

Fortunately, after they went another mile or so, Sam piped up: "Want to break for the night? I mean, this is where you planned to stop, right?"

Relieved, Darcy nodded and stared up toward the mountain. "I'm sure we can find a cave up here. It'll give us some protection—as long as we make sure it's not already occupied."

"Are we talking bears and wolves?"

Darcy had to hold back a laugh. "Don't worry, I'll protect you. Besides, it's a little early for animals to be hibernating."

They turned off the road near three towering evergreens that formed a perfect triangle. Darcy marked the spot with a yellow twisty-tie.

"You sure about this cave thing?" Sam asked as he pushed back a thatch of weeds.

Darcy yanked her boot away from a greedy vine

and pressed on. "Trust me. These mountains are riddled with nooks and crannies."

At last they made it to a jagged hole in the cliff-side. Darcy threw a few stones inside to wake up any inhabitants. When the kids were sure the coast was clear, they ventured inside.

Their flashlight beams danced over the wet rock. They found their way to the back of the cave, where the craggy wall sloped down into a cove.

"This'll be okay for the night," Darcy said. She dropped her sleeping bag and knapsack and stretched. Every bone in her body was tired!

It didn't take long to roll out the bags and break out the snacks. As they ate cheese and crackers, Darcy unfolded her map. She pointed out Whiterock, then guessed at how far they'd hiked.

"We should be right around here," she told Sam. "And here's Big Moose. If I'm right, it'll only take us two or three hours to get there in the morning."

Sam shoved a cracker into his mouth as he stud-ied the map. Their route followed the edge of the Bitterroot Mountains. To the east was prairie land with scattered towns. To the west—just the moun-tain range and the Idaho border. By Darcy's guess they were near a ring of mountains surrounding Hidden Canyon.

"Hidden Canyon," Sam said aloud. "Looks like we're close to it."

Darcy wrinkled her nose. "It's just an isolated valley. No one's seen it for a hundred years."

"It was just sold," Sam said, explaining what had happened that afternoon in his father's office. "The man wouldn't say why he wanted the land. He acted like a spy or something. Pretty strange, huh?"

"Yup." A yawn slipped out, and Darcy couldn't stay awake a moment longer. She tugged off her boots and slipped into the pocket of her sleeping bag. "Don't forget to turn off the flashlight."

"Right." Sam folded up the map, then stretched out. Once the flashlight was off, the total blackness of the cave closed in around him.

The only sound was the steady whisper of Darcy's breathing. Then a green light winked from above.

"What . . . ?" He bolted into a sitting position, his heart thudding. Darcy didn't even stir beside him. What was that?

It couldn't be a star. Maybe a firefly?

"I must be seeing things," he muttered, crouching down on the rock bed again. But as he settled in, a cold shiver reached up his spine. He had a sinking feeling that he and Darcy were not alone in this cave.

Someone was out there.

6

The squawk of a radio made Fiona flinch. She rolled over against something hard, then remembered that she was in the back of her father's Bronco.

I must have fallen asleep, she thought, rubbing her eyes. In the commotion back at home she'd managed to slip into the back of Dad's car and hide under the thick blanket he kept there. Everyone thought she was asleep in bed. In fact, Mom had stayed behind to be with her.

Nobody knows how smart I am. When it came to snooping, nobody was better than Fiona.

She didn't know how long she'd been sleeping, but Dad was still driving around. Fiona pressed her nose against the backseat. It was still night. Her knapsack and butterfly wings were propped by her feet, where she'd left them.

The radio sputtered again. "This is Sheriff Smoke," the voice said. "Do you read me, Charles?"

She peered over the seat. Dad picked up the walkie-talkie and snapped it on. "Roger."

"We've found a trail that may have been marked by the kids. Seems to lead to the old Divide Highway, about six miles from town. Can you meet us there?"

"Will do."

Fiona sank back down and grinned.

They were getting closer.

A sweet clinking sound chimed.

Sam rolled over, and a blunt stone ridge jabbed him in the ribs. *Ouch!* Suddenly he remembered that he wasn't in his own bed.

What was that sound?

Sam sat up and wrapped his arms around his knees.

It jingled again, reminding him of the wind chime on their neighbors' balcony back in Chicago.

Across the cave, a beam of light switched on. It was Darcy's flashlight. "Did you hear that?" she whispered.

"It's coming from the back wall," Sam answered as Darcy swung the flashlight around. The beam bounced along the ceiling, then focused on the rock wall.

Only, the wall was gone!

The brown rock wall was swirling, like a cloud of smoke. Then slowly, the mist faded away. A moment later the dust formed an arched opening . . . a glowing doorway.

"Did you see that?" Darcy gasped, creeping toward the opening.

Sam clicked his own flashlight on and joined her. "Totally weird. This passage wasn't here before." Somehow the glowing door didn't frighten him. It seemed warm, inviting. Sam was edging forward, toward the panel of golden light, when Darcy grabbed the back of his jacket.

"Whoa, partner. This is no time for a spelunking expedition. You could break your neck."

Sam's feet stayed planted in the cave. But he couldn't resist peering into the warm light. Leaning forward, he dipped his face into the golden beam.

The glittering sight was blinding at first. But then a wide tunnel stretched ahead, rising up for as far as Sam could see. Instead of rock, the walls seemed to be covered with flashing crystals! But the strangest thing was the light. The passage was bathed in it.

"Sam?" Darcy whispered. When he didn't answer, she tugged on the back of his jacket. "What is it?"

Reluctantly, he dragged himself back into the dark cave. "There's a tunnel. Looks like an old mining tunnel. The walls are covered with shiny stones."

"A tunnel?" Curious, Darcy stepped into the warm wall of light and gasped. "It's amazing. How far back do you think it goes?"

"It's hard to tell." Although the tunnel was wide, it wasn't straight. The ground snaked up like a roller coaster, then dropped out of sight.

"Let's check it out," she said, pressing ahead into the gallery of light. "There might be an opening on the other end. And if my sense of direction is right, we're in luck. I think we stumbled on a shortcut to Big Moose."

Fiona's mind reeled with excitement as she slipped on her wings and grabbed her knapsack. Silently she pushed the passenger door open and jumped into the grass. Dad was on the other side of the Bronco, talking with the circle of adults.

This was action! The red and white lights of the sheriff's Jeep washed over the area, bathing the mountainside with eerie light. A deputy stood beside the Jeep, waiting for orders.

Sheriff Smoke and Aunt Pam were there, along with two horses from the Ryans' ranch.

"We discovered a trail in the woods," Aunt Pam explained. "Darcy marked off the way with covered wires from trash bags. It led to that cave." She pointed up the hill.

A cave? Fiona stole away from the Bronco and ducked behind the fat trunk of a tree. Were Sam and Darcy hiding inside? She glanced up the dark mountainside, dying to take a peek. Maybe she could make it to the cave and find them.

"We found their knapsacks and sleeping bags inside," the sheriff said, "but no kids."

"They must be around here somewhere," Dad said.

"Where would they go without their backpacks?" Aunt Pam asked.

"Don't worry, Pam," Dad told her. "We'll find them . . . if we have to turn over every stone."

The adults were about to split up when another Jeep pulled off the road. The driver's door opened, and a big man stepped into the flashing pool of light.

"What's going on here?" he asked, his voice a low growl.

It was that man from Dad's office—Marshall Pride.

Aunt Pam explained about Darcy and Sam camping in the cave. Dad added, "We know this is your land, but—"

"No harm done." The big man pointed to his watch and said something about meeting someone here in the morning. "Just be sure you're clear of the area as soon as you find those rascals," he said, heading up the hill. "I'm going to check out that cave again."

Pride wove around the tall pine tree, then marched on . . . right toward the spot where Fiona was hiding.

Her heart thudded in her chest.

He's going to catch me!

7

"I was right!" Darcy said, dancing ahead through the glistening passage. "The cave is really a tunnel. And look. The wind chimes."

She pointed up to a cluster of icicles that hung over the entrance. It was actually the tip of an evergreen branch, frozen into crystals. "I guess the icicles jingle when the wind blows."

"Icicles?" Sam moved toward the mouth of the cave. Outside, a crisp white blanket covered the hillside. "And snow? It's only September."

"But we're in the mountains," Darcy reminded him. "Sometimes we get an early snowfall." She stepped out of the tunnel and took in the landscape. The night sky was shrouded in mist. The cave spilled out onto a hilltop edged by tall pine trees. Montana wilderness—except for an unmarked path that cut through the woods.

"That tunnel may have saved us a lot of time," Darcy said. "I'll bet that path leads straight to Big Moose."

Sam checked his watch, then looked up at the sky. It was almost 5:00 A.M., but there was no sign of a sunrise. The moon was a watery glow behind the clouds.

"So . . . what do you say?" Darcy edged toward the trail. "Want to follow the path for a few minutes?"

Sam glanced back at the cave opening, then nodded. "If Big Moose is close, we can double back and get our stuff before daybreak."

As they walked along, Darcy realized there were good and bad points about finding the shortcut. There was a chance that she'd be on the bus to Idaho sooner than she'd planned. That was good. It also meant that she'd be saying good-bye to Sam in an hour or so.

That was bad.

She was going to miss her cousin. Boys her age were so goofy, but Sam was all right.

Darcy was staring off into the woods when she noticed the big white mound. "Hey," she said, pausing for a better look. "Check out the snow hut."

It was an igloo. The center was more than ten feet tall—high enough for a horse to stand in. Snow had been molded into a perfect mound, and two windows and a doorway were framed by rough-hewn wood.

"It's probably used by hunters," Sam said.

"Mmm. They're not as dangerous as bears,"

Darcy said. "But they can be just as grouchy."

"I'd rather meet a hunter," Sam muttered. "Bears can kill you with . . . Hey . . . stay back!"

But Darcy couldn't resist a peek inside. Snow crunched under her feet as she crept closer to the hut. At the last moment she took long, light steps and held her breath. Her heart was beating loudly when she peered through the square window. With clouds covering the moon, it was hard to see inside.

At first all she saw was fur—thick, white fur. Then she caught a glimpse of pink. Paws? Maybe a cheek? The creatures were asleep on the floor, soft mounds of white fur.

White bears? But the bears in this area, black bears and grizzlies, had brown or black fur. The animals inside the ice hut resembled polar bears. *Only they were nowhere near the North Pole.*

Just then a twig snapped beside her, and Darcy assumed it was Sam. "The hut is filled with . . ."

Her voice died when she glimpsed the figure towering over her. It was so broad she couldn't see around it. Its arms were raised, ready to swoop down.

Adrenaline shot through her veins.

She got a blurry impression of white fur and sharp teeth before the creature growled. . . .

And swung its claw toward her face!

8

That was close! Fiona pressed against the cave wall. Her cardboard wings scraped against the rock as she backed away from the entrance, where the big man paused. He clicked off his flashlight and waited.

Somehow, she'd managed to steer clear of Pride. He hadn't seen her scuttle from the boulder to an old tree stump. And he hadn't seemed to notice when she'd crept into the cave.

Now Mr. Pride stepped outside the cave entrance, reached into his jacket, and pulled out a small, square box. When he flipped it open, she realized it wasn't a box at all, but one of those portable phones. He punched in a number and held it to his face.

"Pride, here. What's your ETA with the nitro?"

It sounded like Mr. Pride was speaking in code. *PTA and night-row?* Fiona listened carefully.

"Well, you'd better slow it down. I don't want a truckload of nitroglycerin arriving just yet. Not with the welcome wagon here. . . . I'll explain later."

Nitroglycerin . . . It sure sounded important. Fiona tried to lock the word in her brain.

"No, we can't wait for the permits," Pride rambled on. "I'm going to blow a way into the canyon whether they like it or not. Yeah, stop for coffee or something. Kill some time. I'll call you back later."

She was trying to concentrate when the footsteps scuffled at the cave entrance. Marshall Pride was plodding in, the beam of his flashlight bouncing on the walls. He really *was* going to check out the cave!

Desperate for a place to hide, she felt her way along the stone walls. But there were no nooks or crannies big enough for a girl with wings.

Her throat tight with fear, Fiona ventured away from the door, into the darkness. The floor was bumpy, and the only thing she could see was the pool of light from Pride's flashlight.

Her sneaker hit something hard, and she stumbled to her bottom. "Ugh!" The fall knocked the air out of her for a second.

"Who's there?" he growled.

Swallowing hard, Fiona dug into her knapsack, feeling around in the dark. She needed her own flashlight if she wanted to get any farther.

At last her hand closed over the light. Scooping up her bag, she switched it on, and the beam swept through the darkness.

"Hey! Who is that?" Pride called. "Stop! Right this minute!"

But Fiona was already bounding ahead, the light skittering over the rock floor ahead of her. She darted down the corridor.

It seemed like she'd been running forever when she reached the cove where Sam's and Darcy's things were spread out. Two neat sleeping bags. Two knapsacks. A package of crackers. It was definitely their stuff, set up beside a really cool archway. It glowed! The light was so bright that Fiona switched off her flashlight.

She nudged Sam's knapsack with her toe. Where were they? Why did they leave their stuff behind?

"Where are you?" came the man's voice.

There was no time to worry about Sam now. Pride was right behind her!

With a last look at Sam's stuff, Fiona edged toward the sparkling white door and pressed inside.

🦇 🦇 🦇

Blood pounded in Darcy's ears as she and Sam tore down the path. A gurgling roar made her cringe and run faster. The creature was still chasing them.

And it was getting closer.

A monstrous shadow loomed over her. It had the body of a huge person. But those furry arms and claws definitely belonged in the bear family.

Whatever it was, Darcy didn't dare turn around to face it again.

"Hurry!" Sam called, gesturing ahead. "Back into the crystal cave."

Darcy didn't want to go back. But did she really have a choice? When trying to escape a bear, you were supposed to play dead or climb a tree. Well, she didn't have the guts to go stiff in front of this beast. And there was a good chance this creature was a faster climber than both she and Sam.

Her bangs were blowing back from her face as she scampered down the last stretch of trail and ducked into the sparkling cave. The tinkling icicles sounded so sweet and soothing, and for now they seemed to drown out the creature's roar.

They had run a few yards when Sam slowed the pace. "I think we lost it," he said between breaths.

Bending over her knees, Darcy listened and waited. She didn't hear the beast. But she did hear *something*.

Footsteps . . .

And they were getting louder.

Someone . . . or *something* . . . was coming this way!

9

Sam heard it, too. "Someone's coming from that side," he said, pointing toward the dark cave.

They were stuck in the middle.

Before they could move, a curly mop of dark hair bobbed into sight. A moment later, Darcy recognized Fiona barreling through the sparkling tunnel. Her face was smudged with dirt. Her eyes were bright with unshed tears. And over her jacket she had strapped on her cardboard butterfly wings.

"Fiona!" Darcy spread her arms wide and rushed ahead to hug her cousin. "I can't believe it's you."

Sam wasn't quite so tickled. He had a feeling that Fiona had led their parents right to them. "How did you get here?" he asked.

"I sneaked a ride in the back of Dad's Bronco," she said quickly. "He's out there looking for you, along with Aunt Pam and the sheriff."

"Great! Did you tell the whole town where we were?" Sam snapped.

"I didn't tell anyone!" Fiona protested, brushing at a tear on her cheek. "Dad doesn't even know I'm here. But"—she darted a nervous look over her shoulder—"that man is chasing me, and he's scary."

Sam glanced down the passage. No sign of anyone. Just winking, sparkling stones. "What man?"

"Marshall Pride," Fiona said, grabbing hold of Sam's jacket. "He's bad, Sam. He's got weapons. He's a . . . mutation expert. I heard him ask some guy what his PTA was. Then he started chasing me and—"

"What are you talking about?" Sam demanded.

"We can straighten things out later," Darcy said, sensing Fiona's fear. "Right now, we'd better keep moving. And I don't mean back to Whiterock."

Sam scowled at his cousin. "You want to go back and check out the bear hut? Maybe we can scare up the whole den this time."

"Very funny." Darcy took Fiona's hand and clasped it tightly. "But right now I think the shortcut to Big Moose is our best bet. I'm not going back to my mom. And I'd rather take my chances with a bear than with the man who just scared the stuffing out of Fiona."

But Sam wasn't so sure. "I say we send Fiona back and fend for ourselves. My parents are going to freak when they realize she's gone."

"Sam!" Darcy protested as Fiona's lip jutted out in a pout. "Would you abandon your little sister with some weirdo chasing her?"

Biting his lip, Sam weighed their options. No, he

couldn't abandon Fiona. And like Darcy, he wasn't ready to go back yet. The sooner they made it to Big Moose, the sooner they'd be able to call and reassure his parents that Fiona was all right.

"Okay, okay, we'll try the shortcut again," Sam agreed. He turned back toward the icicle chimes. "But let's try not to wake everything in the forest."

Fiona ran ahead of them and reached up to touch the cave walls. "How come this cave is so sparkly? Twinkle, twinkle little wall . . ."

"It's probably an old mine," Sam explained.

"Our class toured a gold mine," Darcy said, her blue eyes shining with wonder. "It wasn't half this cool."

"But they also mined silver and quartz," Sam said. "And gemstones, too. Garnets and sapphires."

"Maybe they're so-fires," Fiona said, running her fingers over a cluster of crystals.

"Sapphires are blue," Sam corrected. "I think."

Fiona was hopping toward the back of the sparkling cave. "Fiona . . . ," Sam called after her.

"I want to see the jingle bells," she answered.

"We'd better keep up with her," Darcy said, stepping up the pace.

"Fiona!" Sam shouted. "Stop right this second or you're dead meat!" His feet pounded up the rise. When he got to the top, he was relieved to see his sister standing at the top.

"Now you know how it feels to be left behind," Fiona said.

"I'm not falling for that guilt trip." Sam squeezed her arm. "Don't you ever, *ever* wander off like that again."

"Sorry, Sammy-lammy," she retorted, her dark eyes like two shiny brown buttons.

Sam frowned. It was hard to stay mad at your little sister when she pulled the cute act.

🦇　🦇　🦇

There were no creatures lying in wait at the mouth of the tunnel. And as the kids crept past the ice hut, Sam warned the girls to keep quiet. "The last thing we need is that bear-monster chasing us again."

"But I want to see the bears," Fiona insisted.

"Shh!" Darcy hustled Fiona along. "Believe me, *this* you don't want to see."

When they were a safe distance down the path, Fiona broke into a skip. "This is fun," she chirped. "Where are we going? Do we get to camp out? I should've brought a sleeping bag."

"We're not on a camping trip," Darcy said. Patiently she explained her plan to Fiona, whose brown eyes widened with every detail.

"Then we're *all* going to Idaho?" Fiona asked.

"No," Sam grumbled. "Darcy's going to Idaho. You and I are going home as soon as we drop her off at the bus depot."

"But I don't want Darcy to go," Fiona whimpered. "Can't we—?"

"No," Sam said flatly.

"There's one plus about Big Moose," Darcy said, hoping to cheer up Fiona. "A convenience store— open all night. That means Chee·tos, Twinkies, and hot cocoa."

"Scrumpta-licious! I hope this is the right way to Big Moose," Fiona said fervently.

The path zigzagged through the woods. At one point it went along the bank of a crystal clear lake. Its surface was smooth as glass—a giant mirror reflecting the stars. Darcy picked out her wishing star—the blinking green light. "Please, please guide us to Big Moose," she whispered to herself.

As they walked along, Fiona hummed a little song. Sam was all eyes, on the lookout for hazards. Darcy tried to listen for signals from the forest. But she didn't hear the usual night sounds of crickets and rustling leaves. *Are we scaring everything away?* she wondered. *Or are the creatures closing in around us?* She wasn't sure why, but she kept getting a strange feeling that they weren't alone.

At one point she thought she saw a pair of yellow eyes glowing in the shadow of a tree.

Was someone watching?

She squinted, but the eyes blinked shut . . . and there was only darkness.

🦇 🦇 🦇

The bat circled overhead, riding an air current. Nighttime was his time. Darkness was his home.

But they'd disrupted everything with their noise.

Children! Humans! He had heard them from his crypt. Their cheerful voices grated on his nerves. Especially the high-pitched voice of the little one.

He would have to warn the others . . . as soon as his shift ended at the store. It wouldn't pay to lose the perfect job.

Night work. The job fit Draku like a glove.

With a brisk flap of his wings, he soared down into the canyon, planning his attack. . . .

Scheming.

Plotting.

Licking his lips.

10

A bit farther down the trail, the forest along one side began to thin. Through the trees was a pale landscape. At first Darcy thought it was a snowy hill. But the land was covered with dimples and ridges. "What's the deal here?" she said aloud.

In a few more steps Darcy realized what it was. The woods gave way to hills of sand! "A desert?"

"A beach!" Fiona shouted, racing out of the woods. She leaped onto a dune, sending sand flying. "Oooh, and it's warm. But where's the water?"

"Totally weird," Sam said as his feet sank into the sand. "And I'm not sure this path is taking us any closer to Big Moose. Maybe we should head back."

"But I felt like we were getting somewhere," Darcy said. Discouraged, she kicked through the sand and stared into the mist. Off at the edge of the desert she spotted a pointed building. It had a funny shape on top, and it seemed to be made of stone. "Is that a pyramid?" she asked.

Sam squinted toward the horizon. "Sure looks like it. Weird!"

Darcy shrugged. "Maybe some crazy rich guy had it built. He could have had the sand carted in. You know, like those goofy millionaires you see on TV."

"Sure," Sam said skeptically. He pulled off his baseball cap and ran a hand through his dark curls. "But all the money in the world can't change the weather."

Darcy didn't have an answer for that. Why *was* the air balmy and warm once you stepped onto the sand? She stepped back into the woods. Immediately a blast of cool air hit her. "You're right," she said. "There's definitely a warm front over the sand."

"I don't like this place, Darce," Sam said flatly.

"Just a little farther down the trail?" Darcy pressed. This desert area was strange, but she was sure they were getting closer to Big Moose.

Just then Fiona scampered back onto the trail. "When are we getting to the 7-Eleven?" she demanded. "I want ice cream, I want cake. I want cookies, soft and baked. I want candy, I want—"

"Okay, okay! We're going," Sam cut her off.

They followed the trail over three more switchbacks, and suddenly there was another break in the woods. Through the clearing they could see the sprawl of the town below.

It was an old western town with a wide main

street. There was a steepled church with a sprawling graveyard, a jailhouse, a saloon, a blacksmith's shop, and a general store.

"That's not Big Moose," Darcy said. "At least not the way I remember it. Where's the bus depot? And the Mangy Moose Inn? There used to be a health club. . . ."

"Maybe we found a ghost town," Sam suggested.

"Except for one thing." Fiona pointed to the end of the old strip, where a green and red sign glowed in the night. "How many ghost towns have 7-Elevens?"

She's right, Darcy thought, glancing at the familiar sign. "At least we got one thing right. Let's stock up on food, then blow this popsicle stand."

"As long as we make it fast and keep a low profile," Sam added. "People might wonder what three kids are doing wandering around in the dark."

"Can't we just tell them to mind their own business?" Fiona asked.

"Not really," Sam replied. "We're all under eighteen, squirt."

"My navigation must be off," Darcy said as they made their way down the street. "I was *sure* we'd hit Big Moose."

"Maybe we're in Hidden Canyon," Sam said.

Darcy shook her head. "Are you kidding? Nobody's been in the canyon for a hundred years."

"Well, this place isn't exactly on the cutting

edge," Sam pointed out. He paused at a water pump outside the blacksmith's shop and gave it a crank. The handle came off in his hands.

"But some of the shops look new," Fiona said.

There was a diner, a bookshop, and a haircutting salon. But their names . . . the Dead-End Diner. The Poison Pen Bookstore. And the salon?

"If Looks Could Kill?" Darcy said aloud. "Someone in this town has a strange sense of humor."

"A real comedian," Sam said uneasily.

They passed the deserted jailhouse and stepped into the pool of light from the 7-Eleven.

"Finally," Fiona said. A triumphant smile lit her face as she pushed open the door. Sam followed her in, watching her wings twitter behind her.

Darcy felt relieved to be back in civilization—until she stepped into the store.

The aisles glowed red from the colored overhead lights. The wood floors creaked underfoot. And a chilling mist spilled out from the refrigerator cases.

"Walk this way," Sam joked, limping down the aisle like a monster.

Fiona laughed, but Darcy followed in silence. What if this place wasn't a joke? "I'll get the cocoa," she told Sam and Fiona. "You guys hit the snack aisle."

"Right." Sam guided Fiona toward the snacks.

Quickly, Darcy found the coffee counter. She filled three cups with hot water and poured in cocoa mix. As she was stirring, she noticed the

Slurpee machine behind the counter. A crimson red, icy mixture swirled behind the glass. It was so . . . red. Although the sign said Very Cherry, it reminded Darcy of . . .

Blood.

Darcy shivered as she fumbled with the plastic lids. This place gave her the creeps.

In the snack aisle, Sam was trying to keep Fiona from grabbing everything in sight when he backed into something solid . . . and warm.

"Excuse me," he said automatically. He turned and found himself face-to-face with a ghoulish man.

The man's face was a waxy white mask under a crown of jet black hair. "You don't belong in this store!" he barked.

"You . . . *you're* the clerk?" Sam asked.

"How did you get here?" the man wheezed. "Why did you come?" His dark eyes burned with fury.

"We came for Twinkies," Fiona answered cheerfully, drawing a scowl from the clerk. She folded her arms over the crinkling snack bags and shrank behind Sam.

"Get out!" the man snarled. "Leave this place. And never come back. Do you hear me?"

This guy definitely doesn't like kids, Sam thought. "We're outta here," he agreed, grabbing his sister by the sleeve. "We'll just pay for this stuff."

The crazy clerk was about to lunge at them when

Sam pulled Fiona behind a mountain of cereal boxes and dragged her down the aisle.

"What's his problem?" Fiona asked.

"Don't ask." Sam hustled toward the counter, nearly knocking Darcy over on the way.

"What's wrong?" Darcy whispered, cradling the cardboard tray of cups.

"We've been asked to leave." Sam fumbled for his wallet and tossed a few bills on the counter.

"I'm way ahead of you." Fear sparkled in Darcy's blue eyes as she pivoted toward the door.

Sam glanced behind him. No sign of the clerk. Just a black, rubbery object hovering over by the frozen food section. It flapped like a frenzied bird . . . then skimmed the snack aisle, sailing toward him.

Fiona blinked up at it. "It's a . . . it's a . . ."

A bat! Sam realized as the creature let out a shrill squeal, then dived . . .

Straight down into the curls of Fiona's head!

11

"Aaaarrrggghh!" The snack bags slid to the floor as Fiona waved her arms, swiping at the fluttering bat.

The rubbery black wings flapped madly. The creature's tiny legs clawed at her head.

Sam sprang to action. Grabbing a string mop from the household aisle, he lifted it like a sword. "Back off!" he shouted, jabbing at the bat's body.

"Waaaawww!" the bat shrieked. Its wings flapped furiously, tangling in the strings.

The diversion was just what Fiona needed. She crawled to the end of the aisle, then ran to the door.

Sam dropped the mop and raced out of the store, picking up the box of Twinkies along the way. Outside, the night air was a welcome relief.

Fiona was wrapped in Darcy's arms, trembling.

"Are you okay?" Sam asked his little sister.

Her chin wobbled slightly, and she was trying to hold back tears. "He didn't hurt me," she whimpered.

60

Darcy patted Fiona's shoulder. "Poor kid." She handed her cousin a cup of cocoa while Sam loaded the box of Twinkies into Fiona's knapsack. Then the threesome headed back down the main street.

As Sam sipped his hot chocolate, a weird thought niggled at him. Bats usually didn't attack people. And the nasty clerk had disappeared just before the bat flew into sight.

Had he turned into a bat? A . . . vampire bat?

Way to go, Mackie. Now you're thinking that vampires really exist. This strange town was making him a little nuts. First white bears in a snow hut. Then a sand dune. Now a vampire bat?

It was definitely time to head home.

"We'd better make a beeline back to that tunnel," Sam said. "The sun will be up soon. And I'd rather not run into anyone else in this ghost town."

As they were passing the graveyard, Fiona reached her hand out to the wrought-iron fence. "I wouldn't mind exploring more. Especially since this place is going to get ruined by Marshall Pride."

"What?" Sam squinted. "Who told you that?"

"I tried telling you before," Fiona protested. "Marshall Pride is a . . . a *mutations* expert."

"Mutations?" Darcy's nose wrinkled. "Are you sure, Fee?"

Fiona nodded. "Myou-tations. Yup. That's what they said. And I heard Pride ask some guy about his PTA. And he said something about night-row. *I* think he was talking in code."

"Hmm." A thoughtful look crossed Darcy's face. "I wonder what it all means."

Sam rolled his eyes. He'd been through stuff like this with Fiona a million times before. She had a tendency to get words mixed up. "Night-row. What's that? A rowboat ride after dark?" Sam snorted.

But Fiona stopped walking and pressed her face between two bars. She was sick of being treated like a pest. She had feelings, too!

"Fiona . . . ," Sam sighed impatiently.

Staring at the rows of white headstones, Fiona's eyes burned with tears. Then, suddenly, one of the headstones wriggled in the grass.

"Hey!" She spun around. "That gravestone moved!"

"Uh-huh," Sam said sarcastically. "Whatever you say, Fee. Now can we get going?"

Turning back to the cemetery, Fiona wiped her eyes and stared at the grave marker. But the stone slab just stood there.

"Come on, Fee." Darcy slipped an arm over Fiona's shoulders. "I've got to get to Big Moose. Remember?"

Fiona pushed away from the iron fence and walked arm in arm with her cousin. "I wish you could stay with us."

Fiona's words cut to Darcy's heart. Last night she'd been filled with a feeling of adventure. Today she felt let down. It was going to be really tough saying good-bye to Sam and Fiona.

"I'll miss you guys," Darcy admitted. "But I can't go back to Whiterock. Everyone at school will think I'm stupid. And my mom will be glad to get rid of me. I'm just one more thing she has to take care of."

"That's not true!" Fiona's curls bobbed as she shook her head. "Your mom was really upset when she found out you were gone. She was *crying*."

"Really?" When Fiona nodded, Darcy's throat tightened. So Mom did miss her. But what would her mom say when she heard about the trouble at school?

"Will you come back with us?" Fiona begged.

Darcy hugged Fiona close. "Let's not worry about splitting up until we get to Big Moose."

"It's a deal." Fiona smiled up at her, her dark lashes flickering.

"Okay, okay." Sam shifted from one foot to the other. All this hugging was making him uncomfortable. "Let's get going."

The girls linked arms, and the three kids concentrated on climbing the hill that led out of town. They had made it to the top of the knoll, just beyond the clearing, when Darcy noticed the rumble. "Do you hear that?" she said, pausing to listen.

Sam's brown eyes were thoughtful as he turned back toward the town. "It's coming from down below."

In a few swift steps they were back at the clearing. Clinging to a sapling, they glanced down and saw golden lights bobbing along the main street.

A closer look made Darcy's stomach twist. Those lights were fiery torches! A mob was streaming out of town, heading up the hill! And from the noise of the crowd, they didn't sound happy.

"It looks like they're chasing us," Darcy said.

"Wow . . . there are so many of them," Fiona said.

The dots of fire were bouncing up the hillside, getting closer.

"We can't outrun them," Sam said. "We'll have to hide in the woods."

The kids darted across the trail and into the woods. Sam jumped over a tangle of blackberry brambles. Ahead of him, Darcy was already sifting through a field of tall weeds.

"Yee-ouch!" Fiona cried. Her backpack was snagged on the knot of a fallen log.

Sam turned back to help her, but couldn't free the strap. "You're going to have to leave this behind," he said.

"But the Twinkies are in there. And my—"

"You can come back for it later," he promised.

"Hurry up, you guys," Darcy called to them. She could see the flaming torches through the trees. The mob was practically on top of them!

Fiona let go of the pack, and Sam grabbed her hand. They scuttled ahead, swishing through the grass.

Hurry! Hurry! Darcy wanted to shout. She was so scared, her heart was beating double time.

Finally, her cousins joined her behind a shrub—just in time!

The mob had arrived.

Their footsteps thundered in Darcy's ears. Why were they so loud? And so fierce?

It was as if someone had declared war.

She held her breath as the first people drew close. Their torches lit their faces. . . .

Their *hideous* faces.

"Oh my gosh!" Darcy's mouth dropped open as she scanned the gruesome parade. They were ghastly . . . scaly . . . festering. . . .

"Monsters!" Fiona gasped.

12

"Shh." Sam squeezed his sister's arm, too horrified to look away from the mob. There were monsters of all shapes and sizes.

Snarling werewolves.

Glimmering ghosts.

Cadaverous zombies.

Rotting mummies.

Witches flew past on their broomsticks. Their purple robes flapped in the wind. Skeletons rattled as their bones marched on.

And when a huge bearlike person lumbered by, Darcy recognized the yeti—the creature who'd chased them away from the ice hut.

Suddenly a hand closed around Darcy's arm. She nearly jumped to the sky—then she realized it was Sam.

"Come on," he whispered, gesturing toward the mob. "Let's see where they're going. Just stay away from the path," he warned.

Crouching low, the kids crept alongside the monsters. The underbrush in the woods was thick, so it was easy to stay hidden. But it was slow going.

Just as long as those werewolves don't sniff us out! Darcy thought with a twinge of dread.

When they passed the sand dunes, the kids were on the wooded side of the path. *Lucky for us*, Darcy thought. It would have been impossible to stay hidden in that desert.

In front of Darcy, Fiona was plunging ahead like a trooper. *And I'm quivering in my boots*, Darcy thought.

By the time they reached the end of the path, Darcy's legs were sore from crouching. But the monsters were still tromping on. They climbed the snowy hill and formed a wide circle in the clearing. . . .

Right at the mouth of the sparkling cave.

"What's going on?" Sam whispered. "Do you think that clearing is ceremonial ground or something?"

Neither of the girls answered. They were too frightened by the creature that finished off the parade. The bony figure was cloaked in a black robe. He held a staff with a curved blade at the top. The hood of his cloak covered his face, but Darcy felt the cold dread that rolled off him.

"The Grim Reaper." Sam swallowed hard. "Also known as Mr. Death. What's he doing here?"

The gaunt figure silenced the mob with a slash of his bony finger. Then he combed the crowd and rasped, "Draku?"

The clerk from the 7-Eleven stepped forward.

His red eyes pierced the darkness. *So our nasty store clerk is named Draku*, Darcy observed.

"You are sure? Positive that you saw . . . *others* in Monsterville?" the Grim Reaper asked. His voice was dry as peeling bark. "I hate to be awakened from a dead sleep for nothing."

"Absolutely." The vampire nodded. "Young, noisy ones."

"I s-s-saw them peering into the c-c-cemetery," one of the zombies hissed. "The little one looks delicious."

"Evil has discovered Monsterville!" Draku cried.

"But he doesn't even know us," Fiona whispered.

Sam covered her mouth with his hand. "Quiet," he whispered.

"Now is the time—before it's too late," the vampire continued. "We must seal the passage before the rest of the corrupt world spills in."

"But there is also good out there," said the furry white yeti. "We all know of others like us out in the world. If we seal off the passage, how will they ever find their way here?"

"It's a chance we have to take!" someone shouted.

"Save ourselves!"

"Stop the evil!" Draku added, and a murmur of approval rippled through the crowd.

"Enough!" G. R. lifted a bony finger. Silence followed. "Marta," he said, turning to the white bear-woman. "We respect your concerns. But this time you are outnumbered. Will you cooperate?"

The yeti nodded solemnly.

"We must pool our powers," G. R. instructed. "That will make the seal strong. No single creature will have the power to undo it."

"Wait a second," Sam muttered, suddenly understanding what was happening.

Even as he spoke, the monsters were facing the mouth of the magic tunnel, pointing at the opening. Their heads were bowed in concentration.

Darcy wanted to shout, jump up, distract them— it was her only chance to keep the passage open.

But already the seal was forming. Red flames shimmered over the mouth of the cave. Then the fire turned into a solid wall of bright orange light.

The cave was blocked.

"How will we get out of here?" Fiona asked, her voice trembling.

Darcy bit her lip, afraid to say what she was thinking. *We won't. We're trapped!*

13

Once the seal was in place, the monsters scattered. The yeti headed toward the ice hut. The monsters who could fly took to the sky to avoid the crowded trail. Darcy noticed that the others headed toward town. What had that vampire called it?

Monsterville. A fitting name for a town of ghouls and beasts.

"We've got to figure a way through that seal," Sam said. He and Darcy moved toward the cave entrance, and the orange seal began to hum with electrical energy.

"Sam," Fiona called from behind them. "You said I could get my knapsack. Can we go now?"

"Getting through this seal is a little more important right now, Fee," Sam called over his shoulder. "I don't know if you picked up on what those monsters were saying, but *we're* the reason they sealed off the cave."

"But there are *Twinkies* in my bag," Fiona protested. "I need it. Now."

This time Sam ignored her. "Maybe it only works one way," he said, stepping toward the glowing orange light. "Maybe it just keeps people out." He pressed his hand into an orange ray. Instantly a shiver rippled up his arm.

"Sam . . . ," Darcy gasped. "Your hair's standing out straight—like a porcupine!"

A cold feeling seeped through him, but Sam pushed on. He leaned forward until his whole arm was buried in the orange seal. *I can get through this!* He gritted his teeth. *It's not solid. It won't stop me.*

But the chilly waves of energy grew stronger. His veins were icing over. Soon he was shivering so violently he could barely stay on his feet.

"Sam!" Darcy called. Her voice seemed to come from the end of a long tunnel. "Sam!"

Suddenly he collapsed, and the frosty feeling broke off like a chip of ice. His face pressed into the snow, Sam took a deep breath. Even the frozen dirt seemed warm compared to that seal.

"Are you okay?" Darcy was kneeling over him.

Sam blinked. "That seal is like permafrost."

"Don't try that again," Darcy warned. "Let's see if we can use something else to break through."

Sam sat up and rubbed his palms together. "Good idea, Darce."

They started with a snowball and a twig. But when they tossed the objects into the orange archway, they bounced back out at them—completely coated with ice.

"Weird," Darcy said, nudging the glazed snowball with the toe of her shoe. "Sort of like Jack Frost with a boomerang."

Sam refused to give up. He threw in a rock. He tried a pine branch. And Darcy helped him hoist in a dead log. But all three things came bouncing back out.

"This could be dangerous," he said. "There's got to be something that—"

"No way," a voice chirped. "You're goners."

The kids turned away from the cave entrance . . . but there was no one behind them.

"You're here to stay, buds. Welcome to Monsterville."

Darcy's freckled nose wrinkled in confusion. "Who said that?" she asked Sam.

"Up here!" the voice squeaked. "Boy, you humans really have narrow vision. If you looked up once in a while, maybe you'd learn to fly."

A green light glimmered from the branch of an oak tree. *No*, Darcy thought, narrowing her eyes, *it's not a light. It's an insect. A glowing butterfly.*

The creature's golden wings flapped frantically as she buzzed down to the kids' level. She had chestnut brown hair and the face of a girl. On closer look, Darcy realized that she had the body of a girl, too—slender arms and long, muscular legs. But her entire body was the size of a fist.

"What are you, a firefly?" Sam asked.

"What are you, a bug expert?" the creature

snapped. "I'm a fairy, you dopes. My name is Francie."

"A fairy?" Sam swallowed back a smirk. "You're the one who trades cash for old teeth?"

"Not the tooth fairy!" Irritated, Francie buzzed around Sam's head until he ducked away. "You're pretty gutsy for a kid who's sealed into a monster kingdom. Especially when you're minus one little sister."

"Fiona?" Sam's head whipped around. "She was sitting in the clearing a second ago. Fiona!"

"Where is she?" A sick feeling pinched Darcy's stomach as she searched the base of a nearby pine tree.

"Don't bother looking," Francie said. "She's long gone."

14

"Oh my gosh!" Darcy clapped her hands to her face.

"Not again!" Sam raked the curls off his forehead. "What was going through her pea-brain this time?"

"I saw her heading down the trail," the fairy said. "Maybe she was running away from *you*, Einstein. It's not easy to hang with a guy who knows everything."

Darcy stepped between Sam and Francie and appealed to the fairy. "Can you help us find her . . . please? I mean, do you grant wishes?"

"I'm no genie, but I can fly ahead and scout her out." Francie's green eyes warmed. "I'll do it for you, Darce, since Einstein obviously doesn't need my help. He's got the whole thing figured out."

"Thanks," Darcy said. The word seemed to fly away on the breeze, along with the glimmering green fairy.

"What a pain in the neck," Sam muttered as he and Darcy hurried down the trail.

"I think she's cute," Darcy protested.

Sam just frowned and stepped up the pace.

🦇 🦇 🦇

Fiona yanked her ankle away from a vine and sighed. It would be so much easier to use the trail. But she could hear Sam's voice in her head, nagging: *It's too dangerous. You might run into one of the monsters!*

At this point a monster would make a better friend than her brother. Why did he have to pick on her? And he always forgot his promises. Like going back for her knapsack.

Well, this time I'll prove that I can take care of myself. She'd made it past the sand dunes without being noticed. And just beyond the brambles ahead was the old log where she'd left her knapsack. She was determined to untangle it and run back to the clearing before Sam and Darcy even missed her.

Stepping carefully around the thorny bushes, she glimpsed the red corner of her satchel. But what was that round white thing beside it?

A few steps closer and Fiona saw it move. It was a little white bear, poking around inside her knapsack!

"Hey!" she yelled. "Cut that out!"

The creature turned around, and she blinked. It wasn't a bear. Its face and chest were pink like a boy. But instead of hands, it had paws. And right now, one of those paws clawed her knapsack. The bear-boy grinned, then darted off into the woods—taking the knapsack with him.

"That's mine!" she shouted after him.

But he didn't seem to care. He zipped through a field of wildflowers, then cut between two trees.

Fiona was hot on his heels. She wasn't going to let some teddy bear pull a fast one on her.

* * *

"Leave it to Fiona to make a bad situation worse," Sam said. "Wandering off in a town full of monsters."

"You're just upset," Darcy said. "We'll find her soon." But her words sounded hollow, and that sick feeling was turning into a real stomachache. "I wonder if Francie had any luck."

An hour had passed since they'd first noticed Fiona was gone. Assuming that she'd gone back for her knapsack, they'd hurried down the trail.

But both Sam and Darcy had been shaken by what they'd found . . . or what they *hadn't* found. Fiona's knapsack was gone. And there was no sign of which direction she might have taken.

They'd continued down the trail, all the way to the edge of town. As she hiked along, Darcy had watched the sky for Francie. But there was no sign of the fairy, either. Now, outside the iron gate to the cemetery, Sam paused.

"Why are we stopping here?" Darcy whispered, as though the dead could hear her.

"I don't know," Sam said. "Fiona was so curious about that moving gravestone. I thought she might have come back to check it out."

"Good thinking," Darcy said encouragingly. She could tell Sam was feeling bad: guilty about the way he'd snapped at Fiona and worried about what might have happened to her. Darcy pushed the iron gate, and it creaked open. "Let's take a look."

"I'll go first," Sam said, taking charge again.

Darcy didn't mind. She crept along behind him, chilled by the eerie mist that hung over the cemetery.

Sam moved behind a dark marble slab. The fog was so dense here that it seemed to swallow him up.

Staring through the mist, Darcy lost track of her cousin for a second. When she finally found him again, she stepped toward him. . . .

And he sank down and disappeared!

"Ugh!" A grunt came back to her as she rushed ahead frantically.

"Sam? Where are yooouuu?" Her voice rang out as the earth gave way beneath her. Suddenly she was falling, sliding down into darkness. Her arms flailed as she felt for a handhold. Was she falling into a grave?

But the only answer was the echo of her own voice crying, "Helllp!"

15

Darcy slid down feetfirst until she landed on a soft mound of dirt. The smell of wet earth hit her nostrils as her fingers sank into the soil.

"Darce?" Sam hissed. "Are you okay?"

"I think so," she whispered. "Did we fall in a grave?" Her eyes were adjusting, and she could make out rows of rectangular boxes—coffins.

"Too big to be a grave." Sam slid off the mound of dirt and stepped over to a coffin.

Darcy stood up, rubbed her bottom, and followed. A molded cast decorated the casket lid. Moving closer, Darcy recognized the shape of a man. It looked like his body was pressing its way up through the surface.

"We're in an underground vault," Sam explained. He nodded at the slide over the pile of dirt. "I guess we fell down some kind of delivery chute."

"For the coffins?" Darcy shivered, then rubbed her arms. "Totally creepy. Let's get out of here."

"The chute is too slippery to climb," Sam said. "But there might be a staircase behind one of those doors." He pointed to the far side of the vault, where three doors lined the wall.

Quietly, the kids filed past a row of coffins. *I wonder which door is the right one*, Darcy thought. *And what's behind the other two?*

They were halfway across the room when the molded shapes atop the caskets began to move. . . .

And gory corpses came to life.

"We're in a giant grave!" Darcy exclaimed as she looked around frantically.

A headless corpse marched toward them. A woman with long tangled hair pulled a knitting needle from her neck and pointed it at them.

"We don't like to be so rudely awakened," growled a man clutching a bloody knife. "We need our sleep."

"Our *beauty ssssleep*!" hissed a woman with snakes on her head.

"Don't wake the dead," someone grumbled. "Don't wake the dead."

The other ghosts joined in.

"Don't wake the dead!" they chanted. *"Don't wake the dead. Don't wake the . . ."*

"We didn't *mean* to wake you," Darcy said, edging closer to Sam. He steered her toward the wall lined with doors. "We just fell in. It was a mistake."

Her words sounded so lame! This wasn't like weaseling out of a homework assignment. This was serious!

Sam tugged her against the wall, and Darcy felt the frame of a door behind her. Escape . . .

"Sorry, people," Sam told the ghosts. "Next time we'll wait for an invitation." That was the cue. He tugged open the door, then spun around and . . .

Stared death in the face.

The Grim Reaper stood in the doorway. His arms were folded. His face was a shadowed mask.

"Consider yourself invited," he rasped. "The pleasure will be all mine."

🦇 🦇 🦇

Francie looped over the woods for the umpteenth time. She'd finally found Fiona, frolicking in the woods with Dee, one of Marta's kids. It looked like they were having a blast.

But I've lost track of Sam and Darcy. Where are they?

She swooped down over the center of town. Uh-oh. Trouble on Main Street. Monsters were gathered in front of the old general store. And Draku was at the heart of things. But that was no surprise. A drop of rain and that yellow-bellied vampire would tell you the sky was falling.

Francie buzzed down and landed on a hitching post.

"I'm telling you, we're not safe!" Draku cried. "Monsterville is in serious jeopardy."

"What now, Draku?" asked one of the witches.

The other creatures, two werewolves and a gaggle of skeletons, pressed closer.

"The humans have struck again. First they made off with a box of Twinkies from my store. Now they've kidnapped Dee, Marta's child."

Kidnapping? Francie's ears perked up. That wasn't the way it had looked when she flew by.

"Are you sure?" a skeleton rattled. "Marta has so many children. How can she tell that one's missing?"

"Kidnapping is serious," said a witch named Warta. Francie recognized her by the lumps covering her face.

"Rrreally?" growled one of the werewolves. "Draku tends to exaggerate things. There's never been a kidnapping in Monsterville. Besides, I was just in the store and someone left these on the counter." He waved the dollar bills in his clawed hand. "So much for your stolen Twinkies, Draku."

"But the boy-bear is missing!" Draku insisted. "Stolen away by the intruders. Who knows what terrible things they'll do. They're humans! We've all seen the news reports of their crimes on TV."

A murmur of concern rippled through the group.

"But, but, but—," Francie began. Her green light blinked wildly as she flew through the group. But everyone was talking at once. No one would listen.

"We'd better fill in G. R.," shouted Warta. "After all, he's our mayor. He'll probably want to organize a search party."

Not another mad mob! Francie's wings flapped in fury. She had to find the kids . . . before the monsters did!

Meanwhile, Sam and Darcy were still trapped underground, backing away from Death. "We don't belong here," Sam said.

"There's always room for more," G. R. replied, testing the blade of his scythe with two bony fingers. It was sharp, all right. The fingers broke right off and fell to the floor. G. R. let out a raspy laugh.

How were they going to squeak out of this one?

Just then G. R. reached toward Darcy. She ducked away, just in the nick of time. But his bony finger brushed over a lock of her hair.

It turned white at his touch. Horrified, Darcy tucked the strand of hair behind her ear and pressed against Sam. She didn't want to have the life sucked out of her!

Behind G. R., the ghosts chanted, *"Don't wake the dead. . . . Don't wake the dead. . . ."* They were focused on Sam and Darcy now. Hungrily eyeing them. Closing in. Surrounding them.

"Don't wake the dead. . . ."

16

Sam's lips were set with a determined frown as he pointed past G. R. at the circle of ghosts. "Don't look now," he said, "but I just saw somebody's head roll down the aisle."

The group of ghosts turned around. Even G. R. glanced away.

It was just the distraction the kids needed. In that split second, Sam dragged Darcy past the Grim Reaper and yanked open the second door. It was a shallow closet, full of scythes and axes and swords. No good.

Sam wrenched open the third door. It led to another vault. Quickly he pulled Darcy inside. Wedging the door closed with a dusty coffin, they took a moment to check the place out.

"There's a staircase." Sam pointed to a portal leading to gray stone steps.

"But we don't know where it leads," Darcy said hesitantly.

"It goes up. That's a start," Sam said. Already

they were racing through the aisle of caskets. They had to get out before another gang of ghosts rose from the dead. Besides, G. R. was hot on their trail.

Cobwebs laced across the stone staircase, and Sam broke through them as he ran up. A shaft of watery light lit the top, and Darcy felt hopeful. The stairs rose into a sepulchre, a vault at ground level. Sam pressed the iron gate, and it creaked open.

They were free!

Still, the raspy voice echoed behind them. "I'll catch up with you later," called G. R. "I always do." His cold laughter rolled through the mists of the cemetery.

Darcy shivered as his parting words haunted her. *"Eventually, you'll be mine."*

"Okay," Fiona said. "Next trick is for ten points and half a Twinkie. Let's see who can turn the best cartwheel."

Dee's pink face scrunched up. "What's a cartwheel?"

"I'll show you." Fiona stood up and rubbed her hands together. She and Dee were doing gymnastics on a bed of pine needles in the woods. Actually, it was a contest. The winner of each event got half a Twinkie and special points.

She'd hit it off with the boy-bear. *After* she'd caught him. She'd had to chase him through the woods for twenty minutes. And even then, they'd had to wrestle for her knapsack. It was because of the Twinkies. Dee had never tasted them before, and he was dying of curiosity.

Now, she turned a cartwheel and grinned at the curious look on his furry face. There was something so cute about him. Half teddy bear, half boy.

"Oh, I can do that," Dee said. He sprang to his clawed feet and turned a perfect cartwheel. Then he did it with just one hand.

Fiona hated to admit it, but the kid was good. "You win," she said reluctantly. "Here ya go!" She held up the Twinkie and took aim.

Dee's sharp teeth gleamed as he opened his mouth wide. A perfect target.

"Ready, aim . . . fire!" Fiona tossed the Twinkie into the air.

Dee hopped up and caught it neatly in his mouth.

"Yes!" Fiona was giggling when a dark shadow suddenly covered her. She glanced up to find a furry creature looming overhead. It was huge. And it was so mad, it snarled through jagged white teeth.

Rows of pointed teeth.

As its claws ripped through her collar and lifted her off the ground, Fiona sucked in a breath and screamed: *"Sammy!"*

17

Sam paused in midstep. Had he just heard his sister calling? Or was it his imagination? "Did you hear that?" he asked Darcy.

"I heard . . . something. But it was faint."

"Fiona!" he shouted into the forest. "Fee!"

Silently they waited. But no one answered. There was only the breeze whistling through the trees . . . and a faint buzzing sound.

Buzzing? Darcy glanced up and saw a green glow skirting over a treetop. "Francie!"

The fairy descended and landed on a smooth boulder. "Where the heck have you two been? I've been looking everywhere. You're in big trouble."

"Tell me something I don't know," Sam said sarcastically.

Francie snapped her wings at him and turned to Darcy, who explained about falling into G. R.'s vault. "We had to fight our way out. And before we escaped, he did *this* to me." She touched the lock of white hair.

"It's sort of punk," Francie said. "Consider yourself lucky that you got away. G. R. usually gets what he wants. He's got a lot of power. That's probably why he was voted mayor of Monsterville."

"You've got a mayor?" Sam cocked one eyebrow. "Don't tell me you hold elections."

"Welcome to civilization, Einstein." Francie glared at him, then turned back to Darcy. "I saw your cousin. She hooked up with one of the Marta's kids. The two of them looked like they were having a blast."

"Where?" Sam demanded. "Where did you see her?"

"In the woods, that way." Francie pointed her wings. "But it was a while ago. They've probably moved on."

"We might as well head over in that direction," Sam said. "It's the only lead we have." He pushed aside a branch and held it while Darcy went by. Leaves crunched under their feet as they walked.

"I'm just relieved that Fiona is okay," Darcy said. "Thanks, Francie. That's good news."

"Now the bad news," Francie said, hovering in front of Darcy. "Draku's hot on your trail. He heard that Marta's son Dee was missing. Next thing you know, he convinced some of the monsters that Fiona *kidnapped* Dee. They're organizing a search party right now."

"Oh, great," Sam muttered. "We've been lucky not to have been caught so far. But with a search party sniffing us out, we're doomed. This *is* big trouble."

"Exactly as I said." Francie folded her arms smugly. "Got a theory on getting out of this pickle jar, Einstein?"

"Would you quit calling me that?" Sam snapped. "My name's Sam."

"I know. Sam and Darcy and Fiona. Three wanderers from Whiterock."

"How'd you know that?" Darcy asked.

"I've been watching you for weeks." Francie's green light blinked. "Don't you recognize me?"

Darcy studied her thoughtfully for a second. Then it came to her. "Are you my lucky star?" It seemed pretty far-fetched, but so did a town full of monsters.

"Bingo."

"You're allowed to leave Monsterville?" Sam asked.

"Well"—Francie's face turned pink—"we're not supposed to. Everyone knows it's dangerous out there. But I love the real world. I miss it a lot."

"Then why did you leave it behind for Monsterville?" Darcy asked.

"I had a bad experience," Francie answered. "Out there, a good fairy's workload is tremendous. There's so much to do. Helping old folks tidy up. Yanking kids out of traffic. But one day I was trying to help some kid with his homework and he trapped me in a jar. Kept me there for two weeks."

"How awful," Darcy said.

Francie nodded. "Total drag. After that I needed to get away. A fairy friend of mine had mentioned Monsterville, so I jumped on a flight to Butte and checked it out."

"You fly on commercial airlines?" Sam asked skeptically.

"Of course." Francie's wings fluttered. "It's a lot faster than trying to go cross-country on these things."

"I wish I were a fairy," Darcy said dreamily.

"I'd trade places any day!" Francie insisted. "I've always wanted to be a girl. Sleep in a pink room. Hang out at the mall." Her green light glowed as she sighed.

"Got any practical skills?" Sam asked the fairy. "Can you break the seal on the enchanted cave for us? We really need to get home."

"Sorry, Einstein," Francie said firmly. "The only way that seal can be broken is by the collective power of all the monsters. We're talking major wattage."

They had reached the part of the woods that gave way to the desert. Sam held his hands over his eyes and stared over the dunes that stretched ahead. "So what's the story with this place?" he asked Francie.

"That's King Ahmose's house," Francie replied. "Where would you expect a mummy to live?"

"But a desert in the Bitterroots?" Darcy probed. "It's pretty unlikely."

"A lot of the monsters brought their own homes here, stone by stone," Francie explained. "In Ahmose's case, that would be grain by grain, too."

"And all this stuff was moved in without anyone noticing it?" Darcy found it hard to imagine.

"The monsters used their magic powers," Francie explained. "A lot easier than renting a U-Haul."

Sam nudged the sand with his toe. "I guess we'd better double back to the trail. I don't see any . . . hey! Check it out." He raced ahead and pointed at a dune. "Footprints!"

And they led straight toward the pyramid.

Darcy went over and knelt beside one of the prints. "Well, they're not Fiona's tracks. Unless she has a huge paw with four tiny fingers. Bear prints."

"But she's with that bear-boy, right?" Sam pointed out. "Maybe he's carrying her. She's probably worn out by now."

"That looks like a yeti print, all right," Francie said. She stood in the footprint. The little toe was the size of her head. "But it looks awfully big for Dee. He's only six."

"Everything must look big to you," Sam said.

Francie's green eyes flashed with hurt as she glowered at Sam, then quickly glanced away.

I was just kidding, Sam thought, fighting off a twinge of guilt.

"The problem is, the wind covered up the rest of the tracks," Darcy observed. She brushed the sand from her hands and looked up at Sam. "What should we do?"

He pushed back the bill of his baseball cap. Ahead of them was the pyramid. It looked forbidding, with its stern face staring out at them. Still, the tracks led in that direction.

"I guess we need to follow the trail. Check out the pyramid," he said.

"Not a good idea," Francie objected. "First of all, the yeti might have turned back toward the woods. And second, Ahmose is neurotic about intruders. That mummy thinks anyone who stops by is trying to steal his valuable possessions. Once, when he caught a young zombie near his tomb, Ahmose staked the poor creature in the desert. Left him there for hours!"

Darcy tried to ignore the hot sun beating against her head as she thought the situation through. "I know we're outsiders," she said. "But maybe if you went to him and explained that we're just looking for Fiona—"

"He'd go after me with a flyswatter! That old roll of linen is hyper. You'd better stay away."

Folding his arms, Sam started across the sand. "We don't have a choice. We've got to find Fiona."

"Boys are so stubborn," Francie muttered as she and Darcy rushed to catch up with him.

When they arrived at the pyramid, they found an opening that led to a long passage.

Sam turned to Francie. "If the mummy really

hates intruders, he should close his door."

"It must be a trap," Francie squeaked. "Don't go any farther."

"Fiona?" Darcy called down the shadowed corridor. "Let's just peek inside. We won't touch anything."

"She's probably off climbing a tree with Dee," Francie said, trying to stop them. But the kids were already walking down the shadowed corridor.

"Look at these drawings on the walls," Darcy said.

"They're hieroglyphs," Sam explained. "Ancient Egyptian writing."

"Oh." Darcy thought it seemed a lot more interesting than the squiggles she was trying to learn in school. She could make out a triangle. A hand. A lion. And what looked like a feather.

The hall led to a square chamber with brightly painted wall murals of mythical creatures. Small statues and urns were arranged on stone pedestals.

"It's like a museum," Darcy said. She pressed inside for a closer look at the colorful murals.

Suddenly a horrible grinding sound moaned from the doorway. Darcy spun around. . . .

Just in time to see the wall of iron bars drop to the ground. Clouds of dust swirled up over the gate as the kids ran over to test the bars.

"They won't budge," Sam said. He shoved the bars again, then collapsed with a groan. "We're trapped."

Francie's wings buzzed frantically. "I told you Ahmose was a security hound!"

Darcy gripped the bars. "Can you help us lift these?" she asked the fairy. "Use some fairy dust or something?"

"No way, Darce. I can't undo a mummy's spell."

A second later, Darcy felt a shot of adrenaline as the floor began to rock under her feet!

With a splintering crunch a jagged crack formed across the center of the floor. The floor quivered as the two sides slowly began to separate.

"The floor is opening up!" Darcy gasped.

Cautiously Sam stepped up to the crack. In the pit was a sheet of writhing, hissing, tangled serpents.

"Snakes!" He backed into the bars beside Darcy. "We're going to be dumped into a snake pit."

18

"Oooh! I hate snakes!" Francie's wings buzzed as she looped through the air.

A chill rippled along Darcy's spine. It was one thing running into a snake out on the trail. A pit full of them was too much to handle.

"I must be crazy. But I'm going to try and talk to Ahmose," Francie said. "Maybe, if he's got an ounce of sympathy left in his petrified bones, he'll let you two go." Without another word she zipped through the gate and sped down the corridor.

"Hurry!" Sam's voice echoed down the hallway.

The floor rumbled again, and Darcy had to do a quick step to regain her balance. Discouraged, she leaned against the gate. The grid was wide enough to slip her head through. "Hey . . ." Suddenly hopeful, she turned and pressed herself between two iron bars. It was a tight squeeze, but she was athletic and limber. She angled her shoulders sideways, pushed and . . .

She was free!

"Ahmose's plan wasn't foolproof!" Out in the corridor she raised her arms in victory, then motioned Sam to follow. "Come on! Squeeze out before those snakes get any closer."

Sam pulled off his baseball cap and pressed against the bars. His arm fit through easily. But when he tried to squeeze his head through, his ears got stuck. "This isn't going to work."

"Try again!" Darcy pleaded. "Maybe if you—"

"I'm bigger than you," he pointed out. Behind him, the floor creaked again and the pit expanded. "You'd better get going," Sam told Darcy. "Save yourself. Tear out of this desert, find Fiona, and then get out of Monsterville as fast as you can."

"No!" Darcy insisted. "I can't leave you behind."

"Go!" Sam ordered. "Please."

"I'll be back." She spun around and ran down the hallway. There had to be a way out! Some secret panel or escape hatch or something. There had to be a way to free Sam.

And I'm going to find it!

🦇 🦇 🦇

"Ahmose!" Francie called. Her pixie voice didn't always carry, but it seemed louder in the silence of the tomb.

She'd already flown down a maze of corridors, past two iron gates, and over fiery pits, only to find Ahmose sealed behind a limestone door.

"Ahmose!" she shouted again.

No answer. Well, she couldn't move the door. But Francie *could* squeeze through small spaces.

Buzzing around the edges, she found a tiny crack along the seam. A pinpoint of light streamed through. It would be tight. And what if she got stuck? The idea of being trapped made her break out in a sweat.

But if she didn't do something, Darcy and Sam would be permanent residents of Ahmose's tomb!

Here goes nothing! She took a deep breath, then whooshed into the tiny hole. *Eeeeooouuch!* It was a scrape! But she managed to pull herself through on the other side, feeling a little crumpled.

Inside the dim chamber, Ahmose sat at a high-tech control panel, grumbling, "Thieves! Bandits! Out to rob me of my worldly possessions."

From the back, he was just a bundle of tattered, yellowed linen. Over his shoulder she could see the panel. Two electronic blips on the screen showed Darcy and Sam. A blue square showed the snake pit.

"Ahmose . . ." Francie flew to the control panel and landed on a button marked Pause. It gave off a low beep. On the screen Francie could see that the pit was no longer opening. Whew!

"Who's that?" Strips of linen flapped as Ahmose flinched.

"It's me! Just one of the good fairies." Francie hovered near his face—sunken cheeks and two life-less eyeholes. "I've come to see if you'd soften up and let those two kids go."

But Ahmose wasn't listening. He was too shocked to see a stranger in his command center. "Fairies!" His bandaged hands swatted the air. "Try pests! Do you know what flying vermin can do to my delicate condition? You'll eat through my wrappers in no time."

"Get with the program, bud," Francie snapped. "I'm a *good* fairy. Enchanted dreams? Pixie dust? Any of this ringing a bell?"

"Out! Get out of my tomb! You'll chew through my wrap and nest on my flesh."

"Gross!" Francie groaned.

"Have you no respect for an ancient pharaoh king?" He swiped through the air, knocking her off-balance.

Time to go! "You're a rotten host!" Francie squeaked. Not waiting for an answer, she darted toward the tiny crack and jammed herself in.

So much for that plan! she thought as she popped out on the other side. She'd bought the kids some time. *I hope it was enough. . . .*

🦇 🦇 🦇

Darcy had searched the entrance of the pyramid. There'd been no magic button. No lever. Nothing but square limestone blocks. Then she'd remembered the drawings in the hall.

The hieroglyphs! Maybe there was a message in the pictures.

But as she raced down the dark passage, she felt

a pinch of doubt. *I'm the world's worst reader! How am I going to figure out a message written in ancient Egyptian?* It was one of her all-time dumbest ideas. But when she heard the scraping sound from the end of the hall, she knew she had to try it. The pit was opening wider. If Sam didn't get out of there soon, he'd be dinner for a few hundred snakes!

Darcy ran her hand over a line of hieroglyphs. At least the figures didn't swim and shift around the way words did.

She studied the line of drawings closest to the chamber. A man. Crisscrossed lines. A hand. A bird.

What did it mean?

Maybe the crisscrossed lines meant that the man was behind bars. *The bars in the chamber?*

Darcy's heart raced as she pointed to the next symbol. Was it a code? Was it the key to open the bars, like those trick passages in movies?

She touched the next symbol—a hand. Beside it was a bird.

Oh . . . what could it mean?

Her eyes combed the wall, searching for the bird etching. It never appeared again, in any of the other line drawings.

But I've seen it before. It was etched somewhere else—near the door of the chamber!

She raced to the end of the hall. Sam was hanging from the bars. Only a foot of floor was left. The rest was a pit of swarming snakes.

"I thought you were on your way!" Sam protested.

"No time to argue," Darcy said. "Just get ready to run if this works."

Curious, he set his feet on the ground and watched through the bars.

Quickly Darcy searched the stones until she found the symbol. What had the code said? A hand had been etched beside the bird. She flattened her palm against the drawing of the bird.

Nothing happened.

She pressed it harder. It shuddered.

"That's a good sign . . . I hope."

She pushed the stone again. When she shoved with all her might, it popped into the wall, and a grinding sound echoed through the corridor.

The iron bars were rolling up!

19

"Hurry!" Darcy cried.

Sam was already crouched low, crawling under the bars. Then he scrambled down the hall, grabbing Darcy's hand as he passed her. "Come on. Let's get out of here before the mummy throws us another curve."

Snakes hissed behind them as they shot down the passageway. *I'll be glad to leave them eating my dust!* Sam thought as he lunged ahead.

Everything rushed past quickly: the dark hallway, the limestone blocks of the entrance, the smooth desert dunes. Sand sprayed behind them, but Darcy and Sam didn't stop running until they reached the cover of the woods.

At last they clambered over a few boulders and dropped down onto a bed of green moss.

"I feel like I just ran a marathon," Sam panted.

"Me, too." Darcy tossed her braids over her shoulders and leaned against a boulder. "But at least we scraped by."

"Thanks to you." Sam's dark eyes flickered with admiration. "How'd you figure out which stone to push to get that gate open?"

"There was a message in the hieroglyphs." Darcy explained how she'd deciphered the stick figures.

"Are you kidding? People study all their lives to figure out that language."

Darcy shrugged. "The drawings made sense to me." *A lot more sense than the squiggles and curves of the English alphabet.* "Pretty weird, huh? I can figure out Egyptian hieroglyphics, but I can't read English."

Sam shook his head. "Sounds to me like you have a hidden talent . . . a special ability."

"Yeah, right!" Darcy snorted. "The only problem is that I have to move to ancient Egypt to use it."

"The point is, you saved my skin. Thanks."

"Don't thank me," Darcy said. "I'm the one who dragged you into this whole mess. If I hadn't screwed up in school, none of this would have happened. We wouldn't have forged that letter. We wouldn't have run away. We wouldn't be here, looking for—"

"Whoa! Quit beating yourself up," Sam insisted. "You left Whiterock on your own. It was my decision to tag along."

"And then there's Fiona," Darcy lamented. "I'm really starting to worry about her. She's been gone all day, and it's going to be dark soon."

"Hey, Darce!" Francie landed on the moss beside

Darcy's boots. "I found something that's going to cheer you up."

Darcy blinked. "Is it Fiona?"

"Well, not quite," Francie admitted. "But she was definitely near here. Come on, I'll show you."

The kids followed Francie over a ridge of brambles to a shady grove. The ground was covered with pine needles . . . and a trail of crumbs.

Twinkie crumbs!

"Here's the wrapper," Francie said, kicking the plastic. "Litterbug."

"I'm sure she didn't mean to leave it there," Darcy said, noticing a Twinkie left in the pack. "Fiona would never leave an uneaten Twinkie behind. Something must have happened."

Sam searched the area. "Look at how the pine needles are scattered. I'd say there was some kind of scuffle."

Staring down at the bare patch of earth, Darcy pressed her hand against her cheek. "Poor Fee!"

"What about me?" Francie asked. "I go face-to-face with a paranoid mummy, and this is the thanks I get."

"So you saw him?" Darcy pressed.

When Francie nodded, Sam said, "Is that why the snake pit stopped opening up at one point?"

She nodded again, her wings fluttering. "But I couldn't talk sense into him. The old guy mistook me for a moth. Totally freaked."

Sam grinned. "Guess that's a fairy's occupational

hazard. One swat and you're history."

"Great insight, Einstein!"

"Come on, you two," Darcy said, stepping between them. "We're never going to find Fiona if you guys keep fighting."

Francie hovered in Sam's face a second, then zipped above the kids. "Fine. I'll scout from above. At least up there I won't have to deal with so much hot air." She looped up to the treetops until she was just a flickering green light in the dusky sky.

"Would it kill you to be nice to her?" Darcy asked.

Sam frowned. "Stay out of it." He plodded ahead. The forest was getting dark, but Francie's green light winked above. Man, she could really drive a guy crazy. But there was something about her . . . she was really a fighter.

So why do you get on her case whenever she's around? It was a good question. But Sam didn't want to think about the answer.

20

Deep in the forest, Darcy and Sam felt very lost. Darkness surrounded them. Crashing sounds of thunder echoed from the mountains, promising a violent storm. And Darcy was tired. Each step was a major effort.

Francie's green light was the only glimmer of hope. It flickered above them like a winking star. *My lucky star*, Darcy thought. Though right now she didn't feel too lucky. They were lost. They were being hunted. And they hadn't seen Fiona since that morning.

Suddenly, the green light began to blink frantically. A second later, Darcy noticed other lights through the trees. Yellow dots.

"Torches!" Sam whispered.

Darcy stopped short. It was another mob. The monster search party was coming right toward them!

Francie dived down and fluttered above their heads. "Turn back! Run! You can't let them find you."

Sam was poised, ready to sprint away. "Come on," he told Darcy.

"What about you?" Darcy asked Francie.

"I'll try to throw them off. I can always catch up with you later."

"But . . ." Darcy felt hot tears sting her eyes. She was tired of running. She was worried about Fiona. And she didn't want to leave Francie behind. "Why don't we just face them," she said wearily.

"Are you nuts?" Sam snapped.

"Get outta town, Darce!" Francie squeaked. "You must be delirious. Now get a move on."

"Come on," Sam said, nudging her.

Sighing, Darcy turned away from the glowing dots of yellow light. Pushing herself, she summoned one last jolt of energy and jogged alongside Sam.

But she couldn't run from her thoughts.

You're in Monsterville, said a voice inside. *You can run, but there's nowhere to hide. You'll never escape from the monsters. Never!*

🦇 🦇 🦇

"Hey! What's all the excitement about?" Francie shouted. She buzzed among the mob of monsters, careful to steer clear of their torches.

G. R. led the march. Three witches followed him, darting through trees on their broomsticks. Draku was there, along with a few werewolves and mummies.

"We're on a human hunt," one of the werewolves said.

"They're kidnappers," Draku added. "And burglars. They broke into G. R.'s vault. I hear they tried to rob Ahmose. And I have a sneaking feeling that they have something to do with those thundering noises coming from the other side."

"No kidding?" Francie whistled. "Next time I run into them, I'll be sure to—" Francie stopped herself. *You idiot. Don't tell them too much.*

"Next time?" Draku's eyes glowed red. "So you've seen our prey?"

"Sure," Francie sputtered. She couldn't lie. "I—I saw them earlier today. By the cave." It was the truth. Maybe it would throw the mob offtrack.

"Is that so?" Draku reached out and caught her in one hand. His bloodless fingers clamped over her waist. "I smell a clue on you! You know more than you're telling us."

The other monsters stopped the march to gather around Francie and the vampire.

"Tell us what you know," G. R. rasped.

"Hey! I'm a free agent." Her wings flapped furiously, but Draku wouldn't let go. "Back off!"

But the monsters pressed closer. Their flickering torches cast an eerie light on their eager faces.

"Not until you tell us what you know," Draku said. "Now be a good fairy and lead us to the children."

"No, never!"

The vampire held her to his face, his fangs shining like giant daggers. "It would be such a shame to have to pluck off these delicate little wings."

🦇 🦇 🦇

"I can't go another step." Darcy had been clutching Sam's shoulder for the last mile or so.

"Sure you can," Sam said.

"Nope. I have to rest." She went over to the fat trunk of an oak tree and dropped to the ground. "Can't we take a break?"

Sam shuffled over beside her. He wanted to press on. How could he rest while Fiona was out in the night . . . somewhere? But they were both exhausted. And they weren't even sure where to look next.

"We can rest here." He buttoned up his jacket and shoved his hands into his pockets. "I wish we had our knapsacks. It was stupid to leave them behind."

"At least it's not too cold," Darcy said, yawning. "And that thunder seems to have died down. The rain must have passed over us."

Sam didn't answer. That thunder had a strange ring to it. More like the sound of fireworks. Were their parents shooting up flares to search for them? Geez, they were probably frantic by now, especially with Fiona missing, too.

Nice mess you've gotten yourself into, Mackie.

One of Darcy's eyes winked open. "See those brambles behind you?" she asked.

Sam turned and saw a thick cluster of dark green leaves.

"They're raspberry vines," she explained. "I know it's not much. But right now I'm so hungry I'd eat brussels sprouts if I had them."

Sam reached under the leaves and found fat, ripe raspberries. "Good eye, Darcy." He filled one hand with berries and brought them over to her.

"Suppertime."

"Thanks," she said, popping one into her mouth.

"Now for the second course," he said, returning to the brambles. He ate a handful of berries and sweet juice filled his mouth. How long had it been since they'd eaten? It seemed like years.

A few handfuls of berries later, Darcy sighed. "That was delicious. I never knew berries could be so . . . filling."

Sam settled in beside her. "I'm stuffed," he said, resting his head on a natural pillow of grass. "And tired. But we'd better not stay here too long." He closed his eyes and tried to forget the image of bouncing torches and parading monsters.

They would rest . . . just a few minutes.

Across the clearing, the brambles twitched and shifted.

Their twisted vines began to straighten.

Their green leaves shrank down into a dark cloak.

Their roots hoisted themselves out of the dirt.

And the red berries melted down to pink warts on the skin of a hideous old woman.

At last, the transformation was complete.

"Ugh!" the witch grunted as she shook the dirt from her shoes. Warta hated the feeling of change. But sometimes the only way to do a job well was through a disguise.

And the kids had fallen for the raspberry lure. She threw back her head and let out a wicked cackle.

Oh, those intruders had no idea that the berries were actually a sleeping potion. What did they think? That magic meals grew on raspberry vines?

She waddled over to the two kids and stared down at their peaceful faces. "Gotcha!"

21

"Fiona!" Sleep clouded Sam's mind. And Fiona haunted his dreams. He could see his little sister running through the woods. Her big brown eyes were shiny with tears. But she didn't seem to hear him calling, "Fiona!"

"Stop that at once!" someone ordered.

Sam's eyelids felt heavy as he blinked. A yellow, moldy head stared down at him . . . a mummy! Wrapped in withered linen, its face was a ghastly sight.

"Where's Fiona?" Sam asked. He felt dazed.

"Fee! Fie!" the mummy barked. "Call up that curse again and you'll regret it!"

"Fiona?" Sam asked. "It's just my sister's name."

The mummy's bandaged hands flew up to cover his ears. "I don't want to hear it!" He backed away, and suddenly Sam realized why he was feeling so dizzy.

He was moving.

A cluster of monsters surrounded him. They

were in town, parading down the main street. And he was being carried along on a stretcher.

He lifted his head and spotted Darcy.

Fortunately, she was still asleep. *Good thing*, Sam thought. Darcy had a lot of guts, but she was better off missing this parade. It wasn't exactly fun to find yourself carried along like a roast on a Christmas platter.

Sam glanced over the crowd. *What are they going to do with us?* When he spotted the Grim Reaper at the front of the group, Sam's heart sank. *The old ghoul probably wants to add us to his collection,* he thought, sinking back onto the stretcher.

What he wouldn't give to be lying in his own bed at home. Or hanging out in his father's office. Or even helping out with the dinner dishes.

Dream on, Mackie. The thought that he might never see his parents again left a sick feeling in the pit of his stomach.

The crowd filed through the square, then traipsed into the old jailhouse. Sam lay back and listened as G. R. rasped out orders.

"Put them in separate cells," Death barked.

Sam was carried into a cell and lowered onto a bunk. He glanced up just as G. R.'s dark mask of a face appeared in the doorway.

"I knew we'd meet again," G. R. rasped, then slammed the bars shut.

Sam sneered at him as Darcy was placed in the next cell.

"Time to deputize you," G. R. told a line of skeletons. "Keep these kids under constant watch." He went down the ranks, pinning shiny stars to their rickety rib cages.

"Never thought I'd see this day," one skeleton muttered. "Real, live outlaws in Monsterville."

"It's a shame," another skeleton agreed. "But what do you expect of humans?"

Just then Draku pushed his way in. His cape was balled up in his arms, moving around as if it were alive. "What should I do with her?" he asked G. R.

"Let her go," G. R. said. "I'm sure she's learned her lesson."

Draku unfolded the cape, and Francie flew out from under it.

Francie! Sam jumped to his feet and pressed against the bars.

"You idiot! I could've suffocated in there! I *hate* tight spaces." She waved a fist at Draku, then flew toward the mayor. "And whatever happened to monster rights? Don't they apply to fairies?"

"My apologies, Frances," G. R. said. "But we had to detain you for the safety of our town."

"Wrong again!" Francie flapped wildly. "These kids aren't trying to hurt anyone. Sam is fair and loyal and smarter than any of you. Can't you see that?"

"Save it for the trial," G. R. said dryly.

Sam was surprised at the way Francie had defended him. Despite all her wisecracks, she had a good heart.

"Nice try, Francie," he told her.

"Oooh, they make me so mad!" She was a flicker of green light. "Nobody listens to fairies anymore!"

G. R. barked to the skeleton guards. "Keep close watch on them. We'll begin the trial at noon." He turned back toward Sam's cell and added, "And don't be late. You wouldn't want to miss your own funeral."

🦇 🦇 🦇

Darcy slept through most of the morning. When she finally woke up, she looked around the dusty old cell.

How did she get here?

"Darcy?" Sam called from the next cell. "How'ya feeling?" Quickly he explained how the monsters had brought them here.

"I can't believe I slept through that commotion," Darcy said. "But my head still feels fuzzy."

"Those were no ordinary berries," Francie explained. She buzzed out of Sam's cell and hovered just in front of the bars. "One of the witches laced them with sleeping potion. I heard it all— from inside Draku's cape. That bloodsucker trapped me there."

"What are the monsters going to do to us?" Darcy asked.

"Good question," Sam said. "We go on trial at twelve."

"And what about Fiona?" Darcy asked hopefully.

"No word," Sam answered.

"Oh." Discouraged, Darcy sank down onto the bunk. Trial? It sounded as bad as a test at school.

Francie nibbled her lip. She was supposed to be a good fairy. So how'd she screw everything up for these two kids? Suddenly her eyes misted over.

"Don't be upset, you two," Sam said. "We'll get through this." He reached through the bars. "Give me your hand, Darce. You too, Francie."

Darcy reached out and felt Sam's warm hand close around hers. Francie landed lightly on Sam's knuckles.

"It'll be okay," Sam told them. "And . . . if it's not, at least we're in this together."

Blinking back tears, Darcy squeezed his hand. The last few days had brought so many strange surprises. But the best surprise of all was how close she'd gotten to both her cousins. And to Francie. At last, she had the brother and sisters she'd always wanted.

And nothing could take that away.

"Don't ever forget me," she whispered to Sam.

"Impossible," he whispered back.

By the time Darcy and Sam were hauled out to the town square, the assembly was rumbling with excitement. Every monster in town had turned out for the big event—the trial of the intruders.

Draku paced, his red cape trailing behind him.

Ahmose fidgeted, toying with a loose bandage.

The werewolves snarled as they elbowed one another for a better view.

Witches floated on broomsticks, their cloaks flapping in the breeze.

The faces of zombies and ghosts bobbed in the crowd.

"It's like a circus," Darcy said as the skeleton deputies led Sam and her to chairs on the boardwalk.

"And we're in the center ring," Sam muttered.

Then the trial began.

"Order!" G. R. rasped, holding up his hands.

Instantly, the crowd fell silent.

"As you all know, we are assembled to consider

the crimes of these two intruders," G. R. began.

"They are guilty!" Draku jumped in. "They came to bring evil to Monsterville!"

"No, we didn't," Darcy said, wrinkling her nose. "We came here by accident—through the magic tunnel under the Bitterroots. We thought it was a shortcut to Big Moose."

The group was quiet for a second.

Then Draku countered, "Big Moose? You took a wrong turn. But that's no excuse for your crimes—two counts of breaking and entering. You broke into G. R.'s vault *and* Ahmose's tomb."

"We fell into G. R.'s vault," Sam pointed out. "There was a big, open hole in the cemetery. Some kind of chute."

"Really?" Warta scratched her crooked nose. "What do you know about this, G. R.?"

"It's just a delivery chute," the Grim Reaper said awkwardly. "So that coffins can be dropped off when I'm not at home. Good for business."

"Well, it's dangerous," Darcy added.

"I'm afraid that excuse won't work for me," Ahmose growled. "You walked right into my pyramid. I saw you on closed-circuit camera. I *heard* you talking about my hieroglyphs. You were eyeing my precious artifacts."

"Your statues are very nice," Darcy said politely. "But we didn't touch anything."

"We were looking for my sister, Fiona," Sam said. "She . . . sort of wandered off. We saw tracks outside the pyramid. I thought Fee might be inside."

Again, the crowd grew silent. The creatures seemed to weigh Sam's explanation.

"It's all true," Darcy said sincerely. "We just wanted to find Fiona, then head home." She scanned the group. The monsters were eyeing her as if she were tonight's dinner.

"I must admit, it's a lively story," said one of the zombies. His flesh hung from his cheek as he tapped his chin thoughtfully.

A spindly werewolf sniffed curiously. "I smell a grain of truth in it," he agreed.

Darcy felt warmed by hope. Maybe she and Sam had a fighting chance, after all.

"But what about the young yeti?" one of the skeletons rattled.

"Ah yes!" Draku's teeth gleamed as he grinned at the kids. "The most serious charge. Kidnapping!"

"Has anyone talked to Marta?" someone asked.

"She must be worried sick," a witch lamented. "Probably still out searching for Dee."

"How do you answer?" G. R. asked the kids. "If you set the young yeti free, we will reduce your sentence."

"But we didn't kidnap anyone!" Darcy insisted.

"It wasn't them!" Francie added, buzzing to the center of the square. "I saw the young girl running off with Dee. I flew right over them."

"Aha!" Draku bristled with excitement. "Then we must find the young human!" He licked his red lips, then turned to Darcy and Sam. "In the meantime, you two are guilty of being accessories to kidnapping. You did say that the young girl was your relation, didn't you?"

"Fiona's my sister," Sam admitted. "But . . . please, don't hurt her. She didn't mean to do anything wrong. This is just a—"

Draku interrupted him. "We'll deal with the young one when we catch her. In the meantime, these two get the usual sentence for kidnapping. Three hundred years in the jailhouse."

"But human time is different!" Francie squeaked. "They don't live forever."

"Thank goodness," G. R. said dryly.

"Three hundred is a bit stiff," said one of the witches. "Let's make it two hundred."

"Anyone have a better idea?" Draku asked, glancing over the audience. The crowd seemed unsure. The monsters were still mumbling to one another when Draku clasped his hands together. "That settles it! Two hundred years. Case closed."

"Wait a second," Darcy objected. Everything was happening so fast!

Beside her Sam's eyes were dark with disbelief. "This has got to be a bad dream," he said under his breath. "A total nightmare."

"Take the prisoners away!" Draku ordered the deputies. "Lock them in the jail."

Two hundred years! Darcy didn't want to think about the punishment that loomed ahead. She'd never see Mom again. No more rides on the horses. No chance to hug Gingersnap. No visits with Kate. No more school. *Even English class would be better than sitting in a lonely jail cell.*

The skeletons surrounded Darcy and Sam. They were clamping handcuffs onto Darcy's wrists when, suddenly, the mob parted.

A tall woman covered with white fur lumbered into the square.

It's the yeti—the creature that chased Sam and me. Still, Darcy wasn't sure what all the commotion was about. Then the yeti turned around, and Darcy saw the tiny mounds that clung to her back. Marta was carrying seven white bear cubs. . . .

And one little girl.

Fiona!

23

"Hey, guys!" Fiona clambered to the ground, her dark curls bouncing. Her lips curled in a mischievous smile. "Where've you been?"

"Fee!" Darcy stepped forward, but two skeletons held her back.

Sam managed to break away before the guards could stop him. He rushed into the crowd and lifted his sister into his arms.

Tears stung Darcy's eyes as she watched them hug. After all the searching, all the worrying, Fiona was safe.

The relief showed on Sam's face, too. He still held Fiona tight, her feet dangling in the air.

"You're squeezing the stuffing out of me!" she squeaked.

Sam lowered her to the ground. "Don't ever, *ever* wander off like that again!" he said sternly.

Fiona's nose wrinkled. "Don't be mad, Sammy."

Marta helped Dee to the ground, then addressed the crowd. "As you can see, Dee is safe and sound.

There was no kidnapping. These two scoundrels strayed off together and lost track of time."

Marta explained how she'd caught up with them yesterday. But she was concerned about how the town would react to Fiona. "She may be an outsider," the yeti added, "but she's just a child. Curious to a fault, yet her heart is pure. In fact, I don't know how my Dee would have fared in the forest without her."

"So you have proof that we're *not* kidnappers," Sam announced. His voice carried through the crowded square. "We're just a couple of kids who got lost."

"This does cast a new light on the situation," G. R. rasped. His face was a mask of eerie darkness.

"We never meant to hurt anyone," Darcy said. "Honest. Can't we go home now?" Her hopes soared. . . .

Until Draku stepped close and spread his cape wide. "Impossible!" he snapped. "Out of the question. The tunnel is sealed. Closed! Forever!"

Darcy shrank back from the vampire's glowing red eyes. How could he be so cold? So unforgiving?

But Fiona was undaunted. "Chill out, Dracula." She gave the vampire's cape a tug. "Can you *un*seal the magic tunnel?"

"Why should we?" Draku snapped. "So that you can crawl off to that noisy town on the other side? It's not worth the risk. An open tunnel makes us vulnerable to other troublemakers like you!"

"Now, Draku . . ." Marta stepped up to the vampire. Darcy noticed that she towered over him. "Can't you find it in your heart to forgive these humans? I've noticed that the young one has some virtues. My cubs adore her."

Fiona flashed Draku a saucy smile.

"And I'm sure these two have some merit," the yeti added, pointing to Sam and Darcy. "Have any of you witnessed their virtues?" she asked the monsters.

"I have! I have!" Francie's green light flashed wildly. "They're brave. They never gave up their search for Fiona. Sam would have jumped through rings of fire for his kid sister."

The monsters whispered among themselves.

Please let us go home! Darcy thought. *Please, please, please!*

"It pains me to admit it," Ahmose added, "but the girl is a loyal creature. When the boy was trapped in my tomb, she refused to go on without him."

Darcy beamed as she looked up at the mummy. Suddenly his bony cheeks and dark eyeholes didn't seem so scary. In fact, the old guy was kind of sweet.

But Draku wouldn't back off. "You can't make me like these humans," he sniped. "And you can't make this town open that seal." He crossed his arms firmly as some of the monsters murmured their support.

"I'm afraid this town has lost its direction." Marta raised herself up on her haunches so that everyone could see her face. Her blue eyes were rueful. "Remember why we came here to the Bitterroots? Why we founded Monsterville?"

Suddenly the crowd grew still.

"Each of us encountered problems in the outside world," the yeti said. "Discrimination. Violence. Mockery. Just because we were different."

Darcy frowned. She'd never thought about how it would feel to be a monster. She knew that kids could be really mean to classmates who were different. Imagine if you were a monster!

"We built Monsterville to be a place of tolerance," Marta added. "Our town celebrates the fact that each creature is different. We learned to live in peace. Can't we extend that spirit to these humans?"

For a minute, the mob was so still Darcy could hear her own heart beating.

Then G. R.'s raspy voice split the silence. "Marta has raised an excellent point. I suggest we take her advice. Let's reopen the passage. Send our young intruders home."

Darcy was a bundle of nerves as the monsters debated. A few asked additional questions. Then the monsters talked to one another, their faces alive with curiosity. Finally, G. R. called on them to vote. "All in favor of opening the passage, sound off."

A murmur of approval filled the air, and Darcy's spirit soared. The monsters were on their side!

G. R. smiled. "That sounds convincing to—"

"Not so fast," Draku interrupted. "The seal can only be removed by a unanimous vote." He folded his thin arms petulantly. "And I vote no."

"Now, Draku . . . ," G. R. began.

"Don't try to sway me," the vampire hissed. "I don't agree. I won't agree." He spun around to scowl at the kids. "And nothing you do or say is going to change my mind."

24

The crowd sank back, disappointed.

Darcy's throat tightened as she studied the thin vampire. He seemed to enjoy her frustration.

Just then a clap of thunder rent the air. A second later it was followed by another blast, which rumbled the earth.

"Another storm?" Warta glanced up at the sky.

"That's not thunder," Sam said aloud.

"A disturbance in the earth," said a werewolf, sniffing the air. "Just north of here."

"It's Marshall Pride." Fiona tugged Sam's hand. "He's blowing his way through the mountains."

Sam and Darcy exchanged a look, and the monsters grew quiet again. Suddenly all eyes were on Fiona.

"What are you talking about?" Sam demanded.

"Marshall Pride," Fiona repeated impatiently. "Remember, the guy who bought Hidden Canyon?"

Sam crouched down so that he could look his sister in the eyes. "What about Pride? I know he threatened to blast through the mountains, but there's no way the town will grant him permission."

"He's not waiting for permits," Fiona said. "He was bringing in a truck of *night-row* when I saw him."

"Nitro?" G. R. rasped. "Nitroglycerin?"

Fiona nodded. "He's a m-you . . . munitions expert. Dad says he's going to use the canyon to dump bombs. Mom says he'll ruin the land."

"Why didn't you tell me this earlier?" Sam asked.

"I *did!*"

"She did try to tell us," Darcy pointed out.

"You said he was a mutations expert!"

Fiona shrugged. "How'm I supposed to remember every little thing?"

"Oh, dear," Marta said.

"This is serious," G. R. rasped.

"Our-r-r town is in danger-r-r," added a werewolf.

"We've got to stop Marshall Pride." Sam stood up and addressed the crowd. "We can do it, if you let us go back through the tunnel."

"This could be a trick," Draku accused. "A ploy to make us send them home."

"This is for real," Sam said. "If Pride has his way, your town *and* ours will be at risk. Let us go back. Pride is breaking the law. We can stop him. My dad's a lawyer, and he knows a lot of powerful people."

The thundering roar that echoed through the canyon sent Ahmose stumbling into a group of bewildered zombies. The werewolves howled, and the witches huddled together on their brooms.

The blast was enough to shake up even Draku. "All right, all right!" he said, clasping his pale hands over his ears. "I'll agree to unseal the passage if you can put an end to this bloody noise."

G. R.'s bony fingers motioned wildly toward the trail. "Everyone—to the cave."

Fiona danced Dee around. "We're going home!" Her butterfly wings flapped. "We're going home!"

"Easy, Fee," Sam hushed his sister. Normally they would have celebrated, but this was a hollow victory. Especially with Pride blasting away as they spoke.

"We'd better move fast," Darcy told Sam as another bang sounded in the distance. "Or that man is going to blow this place to smithereens."

*   *   *

As they reached the snowy area around the tunnel, Francie motioned Darcy aside. "I guess this is good-bye," the fairy said softly.

"What do you mean?" Darcy's nose wrinkled in confusion. "Aren't you coming back with us?"

The fairy fluttered down to her shoulder. "That wouldn't be a good idea. Your problems are solved.

And . . . well . . ." Her green glow faded. "Considering the way I feel about the real world and about . . . well . . ."

"And about Sam," Darcy added.

"You noticed?" Francie's tiny face turned red.

"I'm not blind." Darcy smiled. She'd seen the way her cousin always looked at Francie. He acted different when she was around. "So . . . you're coming along?"

But Francie shook her head. "I can't." Her eyes were bright with tears. "I mean, what's the point of living in the real world if you're not a real girl?"

Darcy wanted to argue. But before she could say another word Francie tossed a handful of fairy dust over her and flew off to Sam.

"Oooh!" Darcy couldn't help but giggle as the glittering specks fell on her. Fairy dust tickled!

Sam was sitting on a boulder beside the cave entrance when Francie buzzed over. "Adios, Einstein."

"What's that supposed to mean?" he asked.

"This is the end of the line." Francie landed on the boulder and pointed a wing at the tunnel entrance. "I can't go back with you."

"But you said you like the real world. You said—"

"I said that I always wanted to be a real girl," Francie pointed out. "And it's time that I gave up wanting something I can't have. I'm a fairy. A pesky insect. An oversized flying—"

"No!" Sam said. "You're better than that. You

may be a lightweight, but you've got the power of a hundred girls. The way you stood up to those other monsters . . . I don't know any girl with the courage to fend off a vampire and the Grim Reaper."

"Thanks for the vote of confidence." Francie's cheeks were tinged with pink. "I won't forget you, Sam." Her green light flashed as she floated above his head, then flew into the crowd.

G. R. called the monsters to attention. "Is everyone ready?" Behind him, the orange seal glowed in the archway.

Marta bent down and kissed the top of Fiona's head. Then she patted her behind and pushed her ahead.

Sam's eyes were stormy as he joined Darcy and Fiona. He couldn't shake the feeling that he'd just lost a good friend. *I've got to stay focused. The important thing is getting back to Whiterock to stop Marshall Pride.* He pulled his cap down and nodded at G. R.

The monsters formed a semicircle around the cave. Quiet now, they stared at the orange seal. Darcy watched for signs of magic, but everything seemed normal. Then, suddenly, the orange glow went bright red. It exploded with a loud pop, then fizzled away.

"Cool!" Fiona tugged on Darcy's hand. "Let's go."

"Good-bye!" Darcy called to the monsters. Her eyes skimmed over their faces. Where was Francie?

"Don't forget your promise," Draku called as the

kids waved one last time and ducked into the cave. "Stop that man and those dreadful explosions."

Inside, the walls twinkled around them.

"It's still sparkly," Fiona said excitedly. "This has been the best trip ever. Can we come back here again, Sammy-lammy?"

"No," he said sullenly. His feet scraped over the ground as he walked.

Darcy could tell he was upset, and she understood why. Sam had gotten attached to Francie—more attached than he'd admit.

Just then Darcy heard a noise from the tunnel.

"What was that?" Sam stopped short and stared ahead. Someone was in the tunnel, running toward them.

"Who's there?" Darcy called out.

Sam squinted into the light. The large man stood out against the white cave walls. Sam could make out his square jaw . . . and his sunglasses. "Marshall Pride!"

25

Darcy gasped. "But he's been blasting north of here. How did he find his way into the cave?"

Sam glanced up at the approaching man, then back at the girls. "Not a word about Monsterville," he whispered. "We've got to get him to turn back."

"Hello in there!" the man called. He barreled along, pounding to a stop in front of the kids. "You're Charles Mackie's boy," he said, studying Sam.

Sam nodded. "Yes, sir."

Pride looked around. "This little tunnel is a real spectacle. I should organize a tour." He looked back at the kids and frowned. "But your parents have a search party combing the mountains for you. The whole sheriff's department. Horses and helicopters!"

"We got lost," Sam said. "Can you help us find our way out?"

The man gave them a guilty look, then glanced ahead. From his greedy smile, Darcy could tell he wouldn't turn around. "You just head out that way," Pride said, pointing behind him. "You'll find a few men from my crew outside the cave there. They'll radio the sheriff for you."

"It doesn't go through," Sam said.

Picking up on his plan, Darcy added, "You shouldn't go any farther. There's . . . there are snake pits and bears and . . . it's really dangerous."

"Is that right?" Pride patted Fiona on the head, then backed toward Monsterville. "Nothing I can't handle. Now move along. Your parents are worried sick."

"Mr. Pride!" Sam knew he had to stop him. "Wait!"

But the man was already jogging down the tunnel.

"Hey, mister! Come back!" Fiona shouted.

Darcy put her hands on Fiona's shoulders and watched as the man disappeared. "This is awful," she muttered. "He's the last person who should be running loose in Monsterville."

"Like a bull in a china shop." Sam could imagine what Pride would do once he got a look at Monsterville. The guy might give up his plans for a munitions dump and turn the place into an amusement park! The faces of G. R. and Francie and Ahmose flashed through Sam's mind. All they wanted was to be left alone. Instead, they were getting an unexpected visit from a lunatic.

"Come on," Sam said, grabbing Fiona's hand. "We've got to go back and warn the monsters." He wasn't sure if Darcy would agree. But a second later she grabbed Fiona's other hand and nodded.

"Let's go!" she exclaimed.

By the time the kids made it back to the end of the cave, Monsterville was quiet. There was no sign of Marshall Pride. And the monsters had headed home.

"I hope we're not too late," Darcy said.

Breathlessly, Sam looked around. "We've got to move fast. Maybe we should go straight to the yeti's ice hut. Or maybe—" His voice trailed off when he saw a flash of green behind a boulder. "Francie?"

The fairy fluttered up onto the rock. Her eyes were rimmed with red, and Darcy could tell she'd been crying. But she perked up when she spotted Sam. "Hey, guys," she said, wiping her nose on a wing. "What are you doing back here?"

"We came back to warn you," Darcy said.

"You're in big trouble," Fiona added. "Didn't you notice that big guy who just ran out of this cave?"

Francie shrugged. "I was . . . a little distracted."

"Marshall Pride is here!" Fiona sputtered. "He found the magic tunnel."

"Jumping Jupiter! This is awful!" Francie

squeaked. "How are we going to stop him?"

"I've got an idea," Sam said. "But we need the witches. They must have some kind of potion that will make Pride forget what he sees, so Monsterville will be safe."

"Great!" Francie said. "I'll go get them." She shot into the air, a bolt of green light. "Be back in a jiffy."

Within minutes, a squadron of witches came soaring across the sky. Their purple capes swirled around them as they landed in the clearing.

"I told them everything," Francie chirped. "They're ready for battle."

"Not to worry," Warta said, jumping off her broomstick with a thud. "We can take care of everything. We have a brew for people like Pride. We'll just turn ourselves into berry bushes, and when he—"

"I don't think he'll fall for the bush trick," Sam interrupted. "We need a bigger and better lure. Like a mountain of gold or a sea of pearls."

One of the witches scratched a red scar on her chin. "Glitter Lake," she suggested.

"Just what I was thinking, Scar," Warta agreed. She glanced over the squadron of witches. "We'll have to split up. Chortle, Pimple, and Scar will stick with me. Everyone else should fly around Monsterville to spread the warning. Oh . . . and nudge the intruder toward Glitter Lake. A gentle prod should do it."

Without another word, several of the witches

leaned low on their broomsticks and zoomed off.

"We'd better hurry," Francie said, her green light flashing.

"Right," Warta agreed. "We have to get to Glitter Lake before the horrible human does." She swung onto her broomstick, then scooted up beside Darcy. "Hop on, dears. Sam can ride with Scar. Fiona with Chortle. And hold on tight. We'll be flying at top speed."

"Flying!" Fiona jumped onto the fat witch's stick and grabbed the purple cloak. "Can you show me how to do this for the class play?"

"Just hold on, dear," Chortle replied. She leaned forward, and the broomstick whooshed into the air.

This is amazing! Darcy could barely contain her excitement as she flew into the sky on Warta's stick. The wind brushed back her hair. Below her, the forest was like a tiny model for a toy train . . . clean and peaceful. They couldn't let Marshall Pride ruin it all!

The witches flew in formation, with Francie buzzing along at the point. The land rushed past beneath them until, at last, they arrived at Glitter Lake. The broomsticks touched down gently, and the kids clambered off.

"Hide, hide, hide!" Warta ordered. "Into the brambles! Behind the trees. We don't want to tip the man off."

Everyone rushed to find cover. Darcy grabbed Fiona's hand and led her up the hill, Sam on their heels. They sifted through some tall wildflowers, then found a spot behind a fallen tree. Sam and Warta hid behind a nearby bush. The other witches sank behind the ridge of brambles.

Francie buzzed down onto Darcy's shoulder. "I wish I could just sprinkle this guy with a blast of fairy dust," she said. "These spells always make me nervous."

"Quiet, please!" Warta murmured. "I haven't used this spell for years. Let's see how well I remember it." She screwed up her face, then began to chant:

> "DRUMS ROLL! TRUMPETS TOOTLE!
> GLITTER LAKE, COLD AS A NOODLE,
> TURN TO GOLD, THE WHOLE CABOODLE!
> MAKE THIS WICKED MAN TAKE FLIGHT,
> BRING THE VERY CORE TO LIGHT."

What a strange spell, Darcy thought. What did it mean? "I thought you were going to use a sleeping potion," she whispered. "Like the one you used on us."

"And what about his memory?" Sam asked. "Don't you have something that will erase it? If he goes back and tells everyone about Monsterville, there's—"

"Shoosh!" Warta hissed. "Can't you see I need to concentrate?"

Darcy bit her lip. She was beginning to wonder if this whole plan would work. But as she crouched behind the log, pinpoints of light shimmered on the lake.

"Look!" Fiona whispered. "The water's turning colors."

It was true! The water was turning into a huge pool of . . .

Gold coins!

Even though the sky was gray, they winked merrily, as if shedding their own light. They shifted and tossed onto the shore in gentle waves.

"Pretty cool," Sam whispered.

"Shoosh!" Warta repeated. "He's coming. I can feel it."

Darcy scanned the waterfront. Except for the *chink-chink* of rolling coins, the area was quiet. Then she saw a movement at the end of the trail. A moment later Marshall Pride stepped into view.

"Now go for the gold," Sam muttered.

Pride meandered along. He reminded Darcy of a dog, sniffing aimlessly. Then he noticed the lake.

Curious, he squinted, then rushed forward and knelt at the edge of the shimmering gold. He lifted a coin to his mouth and clamped down on it, testing it.

"Good," Warta whispered. "Very good. Now do it again."

But Pride didn't need any more proof. He just stood up and tucked the coin into his pocket, staring at the lake in wonder. Then he opened his arms wide, as if he wanted to give it a big hug.

"Take a dip!" Warta whispered. "A little swim!" She cracked open one eye, then sighed. "He has to get closer to the gold. If he doesn't, the spell won't work."

But Pride wasn't budging. In fact, he was stepping back, moving away from the lake.

"This guy needs a kick in the pants," Francie muttered.

Darcy was about to agree when Francie buzzed into the air. Her green light blinking, she darted toward Marshall Pride.

"What . . . what's going on?" Warta asked.

"Francie!" Darcy called . . . but it was too late.

The fairy was already buzzing behind Pride's back. She rammed into his shoulder, but he didn't budge.

Careful, Francie! Darcy gritted her teeth. Francie was so tiny, and Pride was a big man. He could squash her with one bat of his hand!

Francie circled, her face pinched with determination. She tossed a handful of dust onto Pride's head. The man twitched and started to sneeze.

It was enough to throw him off-balance. Francie fluttered toward him and pushed. There was a tangle of wings and flailing arms. Then Pride stumbled forward.

Off-balance, he slipped into the lake of shimmering coins. . . .

Pulling Francie down into a heavy wave of gold.

26

"Francie!" Sam shouted. He was already on his feet, racing down to the lakeside.

Darcy and the others were right behind him. They searched the lake surface for Francie. But there was no sign of life—just a churning pool of gold coins.

"Oh, Francie!" Darcy fell to her knees. "Where are you?"

"Don't go any closer!" Warta ordered. "Do you want to be transformed, too?"

Just then a screech came from the churning gold, and two black, rubbery wings emerged.

It was a bat.

The crowd watched curiously as the creature pushed itself out of the coins and flew to the shore. With another shrill squeak, it began to twist and stretch like a string of black licorice.

"Is that Francie?" Fiona blinked.

A moment later, the rubbery wings formed a black satin cape. The tiny rodent body popped into a full-size man. It was Marshall Pride. But now his teeth were long, pointed fangs.

"What is going on here!" he snapped. "What did you do to me, you old witch?"

"I knew it!" Warta said. "I knew there was a monster inside him. It was just dying to come out."

"A vampire?" Sam asked.

"Are you surprised?" Warta countered. She sneered at Pride. "You must have sucked the life out of your share of humans. Well, you'll have to learn manners here in Monsterville. We don't look fondly on greed."

"Monsterville?" he snapped. "I—I—"

"Be happy that you finally found a home," Scar advised him. "Don't worry. Draku will show you the ropes. You two should get on just fine."

Meanwhile, Sam was staring at the churning lake. "What about Francie?" he asked. "Can't she find her way to the surface?"

"What if she was crushed?" Fiona lamented.

Warta glanced back at the lake and frowned. "I wish I could help. But it's been so long since I used that spell, I'm afraid my powers are a little rusty."

Darcy's throat was tight with pain. She couldn't stand to think of her friend trapped in the lake, smothering under those heavy coins. . . .

Just then the coins stirred, and a hand emerged. A full-size, human hand.

"Somebody's in the lake!" Fiona shrieked. "A person!"

Darcy held her breath as she stared at the emerging figure.

A girl.

Liquid gold dripped from her narrow shoulders and long, straight hair. Silently she stepped through the coins and walked onto the shore.

She smiled at the curious crowd, and suddenly Darcy recognized the familiar features.

"Francie?" Sam gasped.

She had turned into a real, full-size girl!

"You got it right, Einstein," Francie snapped. "What's everybody staring at? And what's with this stuff dripping all over me. Boy, I feel heavy. My wings must be soaked." She wiped the gold film from her face, then turned to look back at her wings.

They were gone.

"What the . . ." Her face registered shock as she glanced down over her new body. "I'm . . . I'm *big*."

"You're a girl," Darcy said.

"A real knockout," Sam muttered under his breath.

In the commotion, Darcy was the only one who caught his comment. She glanced over at him, and he looked away, embarrassed.

"It's the spell," Warta admitted. "Bring the very core to light. I guess you were always a girl deep inside." She touched Francie's arm. "Will you ever be able to forgive me? I'm afraid your fairy powers are gone for good."

"Forgive you?" Francie wrapped her arms around Warta and gave her a warm hug. "This is the best thing that's ever happened to me. A dream come true!"

"Ooooh!" Warta shrieked. "And I was about to toss out that old spell. Who knew?"

As everyone began to talk and laugh at the same time, Darcy looked over the group. The witches were giddy with excitement. Sam couldn't take his eyes off Francie, who positively glowed with happiness. And Fiona was tugging on Chortle's cloak, eager for another ride on the broomstick.

This place is magic, Darcy thought. She smiled. Wonderful things had happened to them here in Monsterville. It was time to go home. But she would never forget this incredible place.

🦇 🦇 🦇

By the time the kids returned to the cave entrance, the monsters had gathered to see them off. *Word sure travels fast here*, Darcy thought. *Especially when you have a squadron of witches in the air.*

"We heard of your heroics," Ahmose told them.

"You saved our town from that scoundrel," Marta cried, hugging the kids.

"Oh, come on," Pride the vampire said. "I wasn't that bad." His cape dangled awkwardly over one shoulder. And he kept fingering his new fangs, as if he wasn't sure what to do with them.

"Hmm." Draku's mouth twisted in a smirk. "I

142

can see that we've got a lot of work to do!"

"We're going to walk you through the tunnel," one of the zombies announced. "A mons-s-ster es-s-scort!"

G. R. fell into line beside Sam. "You have a great mind, Sam. Keep developing it."

"Thanks," Sam said, still a little creeped out to be so close to Death. "You kept me on my toes. Especially with all those ghouls in your vault."

G. R. grinned. "Quite a crew, hmm? Next time I'll show you the rest of my collection."

"I don't think there'll be a next time," Sam said.

G. R. laughed. "We'll be seeing each other again. I never say good-bye. Just 'see you later.'"

Silently, Sam moved ahead in the crowd. You could never get too comfortable with the Grim Reaper.

Darcy walked along beside Ahmose. The mummy was giving her a quick lesson in Egyptian hieroglyphics.

"There's so much to cover," he said. "The point is, you are a very smart girl. But you process information differently from other humans. Pictures make more sense to you than abstract letters. That's why you find it hard to read in your own language."

Darcy squinted up at him. "Are you saying I should study Egyptian?"

He let out a dry laugh. "If you like. In the meantime, work on your reading. And don't be afraid to get help. You'll have to work hard, but you can do it."

Darcy nodded. After facing a jury of monsters, anything would be a cinch. Even a meeting with the school principal!

"I have something for you," Ahmose said. He reached into the wrappings at his waist and pulled out a thin leather-bound book. A snake and a triangle were etched on the cover. Darcy opened it and found hieroglyphs scrawled over the yellowed pages. "Take it home with you," he said. "And think of me when you're trying to decipher the ancient clues."

"Thank you, Ahmose," Darcy said softly. "I'll keep this . . . forever."

The mummy pressed a bandaged hand to her cheek. His linen smelled musty, but deep inside Darcy knew he had a wise, kind heart.

At the end of the tunnel, the monsters filed out and gasped at the sight of the big blue Montana sky.

"Sometimes in the canyon we forget," Marta said. "We forget that there's another world out here."

"I never forget," Draku said. "I wish it would go away."

"But there are others like us out here," Warta said. "We need to keep the tunnel open, so they can find their way in."

On the ridge below the triangle of pine trees, Sam spotted a black Jeep and two trucks: Pride's crew. "You'd better take cover," he told the monsters. "Unless you want some human visitors real soon."

"Good-bye! Good-bye!" Dee sang to Fiona. "Come back and visit us."

"I will," Fiona promised.

"No she won't," Sam corrected.

Fiona gave her brother a pouty look, then hugged the young yeti.

"Thank you for helping us," G. R. told the kids in his usual raspy voice. "And take care out there, Francie. It's not an easy world to live in."

"I know," Francie admitted. "But I always loved a challenge."

As Darcy waved good-bye, she had a feeling that her adventure wasn't quite over. Something told her she'd see her friends from Monsterville again.

The four kids were hiking down the path when Fiona piped up. "Hey! It's Dad's Bronco!"

"We're up here!" Darcy shouted, waving.

Suddenly, all four kids were jumping up and down, shouting and waving. The Bronco pulled off the road, and out spilled Charles and Lila Mackie, along with Pam Ryan.

"Looks like we've got a ride home," Darcy said. *Home.* How had she ever thought she could leave?

"Mom is gonna kill us," Fiona said, clambering down the hillside. "We're going to be grounded for a hundred years."

"Really?" Francie asked. "That sounds terrible."

"Don't listen to her," Sam said. "We'll be fine. Just as long as a certain someone can keep her mouth shut about what really happened in Monsterville."

"I *love* secrets," Fiona insisted.

"This is one secret you'd better not spread through the whole first grade," Sam warned.

"I can't wait to show you the ranch," Darcy told Francie. "We've got a spare room, so you can have your own bedroom."

Francie smiled. "Is it pink?"

"No," Darcy admitted, "but we can paint it."

"As long as it's no trouble," Francie said.

"Uh, Darce?" Sam said. "How are you going to explain a teenage girl coming from nowhere? I mean, don't you think your mother will be suspicious?"

"We'll work it out," Darcy said. "I could tell Mom that Francie is Kate's older sister . . . that she didn't want to move to Idaho . . ."

"This I gotta see," Sam muttered.

"Don't worry, Einstein," Francie said lightly. "We got this far, didn't we?"

There's more spooky

adventure coming your way in

Don't Go into the Graveyard!

by R. A. Noonan

Here's a spine-tingling preview . . .

2

"A witch?" Darcy asked, staring into the mirror. "What made you think of this? Was it my crooked nose? Or my wicked mood today?"

"You have a cute nose!" Francie insisted. She shoved a black, pointed hat over Darcy's blond head.

"Mmm-hmm," Darcy murmured. "And you just happened to have this costume lying around?"

"I was going to be a witch," Francie explained. "Then I saw those hula dancers on MTV. The rest is history."

Darcy grinned at her reflection and nearly laughed. Francie had given her some tooth wax, and it looked like she was missing a front tooth.

"Nice smile," Francie teased.

The drapey black dress was big on Darcy, but Francie had hiked it up with a belt. A putty wart and ratty broom completed the look.

"Thanks, Francie," Darcy said. She took one last

look in the mirror. "Now I'm getting in the Halloween spirit."

"Good," Francie said, leading the way down the stairs. "I'm going to squeeze the most out of Halloween, or my name isn't . . ."

"Francie *Capezio*?" Darcy teased.

"Whatever."

Francie's true identity was a secret shared by Darcy and her cousins. When Francie had turned into a girl, Darcy insisted that she move in at the Ryan ranch.

"But you can't just bring a kid home," Sam had pointed out. "People will ask questions."

"I'll tell them she's Kate's cousin," Darcy had said. Darcy's friend, Kate Capezio, had recently moved to Idaho. And everyone knew the Capezios had a huge brood of kids.

"What about permission?" Sam had probed.

"We'll get someone to call and pretend she's Francie's mom. She can say something about getting her daughter away from the city."

"Sounds hokey," Sam had objected. "Besides, we don't know any adults who'll make a call like that."

Monsterville to the rescue! Darcy had talked Marta, a huge, snow white mountain creature, into making the call. A mother of nearly a dozen cubs, the yeti had a kind streak. And a very motherly voice.

In the end, Darcy's mom had agreed.

What do you expect from a mom with the biggest

heart in the world? Pam Ryan had taken Francie in with open arms.

Francie had fit in well on the Ryan ranch. She was great with customers for trail rides. She loved to cook. And her laughter was contagious.

Darcy had always wanted a sister. Who knew that she would come from a glimmering creature the size of a lemon?

🦇 🦇 🦇

"It's a Teenage Mutant Ninja Turtle!" Fiona cried.

An odd assortment of creatures roamed Boot Hill. Kids dressed in crazy costumes were scattered among the graves.

Gunslingers joked with aliens.

Frankensteins schmoozed with Cinderellas.

A pirate tossed a Frisbee to Morticia Addams.

Mr. Spock shared a bag of tortilla chips with a mummy wrapped in toilet paper.

"This is like being back in Monsterville," Sam said.

"Where's Mild Cody?" Fiona asked.

"That's *Wild* Cody," Sam corrected her.

"Look at the costumes," Francie gasped. "Isn't it great?"

Darcy had to agree. She felt better already. It would have been a drag to miss Halloween just because of snobby Annabel Mackinac and her dumb party.

Now, Darcy stopped short. Her good mood faded as she glimpsed long, shiny platinum hair.

Annabel Mackinac was here!

Dressed in a spangly tutu, Annabel led a big group of girls in bright costumes up Boot Hill. She'd brought her entire party! And any second now they'd see Darcy.

I can't face them, Darcy thought. She couldn't bear to see the girls' faces. They'd know for sure she hadn't been invited. And she hated it when people felt sorry for her!

Quickly, she tugged her witch's hat over her eyes to shield her face. But it was too late.

"Darcy!" Nora Chambers called. Her braces glimmered in the sunshine, matching her aluminum foil antennae. She was dressed as a bee. Her stinger jiggled as she grabbed Brook Lauer's arm.

"Hi!" Brook called. They both waved so frantically that Darcy knew they must be feeling guilty. Brook was dressed as a princess, and her blond wig almost fell off as she motioned to Darcy to join them.

Annabel Mackinac's platinum hair whipped around her shoulders as she turned to look at Darcy. Her ice blue eyes glinted.

"Come on," she said loudly. "Let's stick together, girls. We don't want any *losers* mixing in with our group."

Darcy's face flushed. Nora and Brook gave her a helpless glance, then followed Annabel and the rest of the girls farther up the hill.

Francie's green eyes snapped with anger. "That girl is a menace!" she declared. "If I still had my pixie dust, I'd turn her into a marshmallow, pronto!"

"You *would*?" Fiona breathed. "Could you turn me into a Twinkie?"

"Don't let her bug you, Darcy," Sam told her.

But Darcy's eyes stung with tears. She knew Annabel was just a mean snob, but it hurt that the rest of the girls had gone along with her.

"Let's get closer to the grave," Sam said.

"You guys go on ahead," Darcy told them. "I'll catch up. I—I have a stone in my sneaker."

Sam started to protest, but Francie caught the glint of tears in Darcy's eyes, and she tugged on his arm. "We'll meet you by the grave," Francie said quietly. She and Sam walked up the path with Fiona skipping ahead.

I need to get away, Darcy thought, swallowing hard. She spied a tall pine tree a few steps off the main path. Its low, bushy branches would offer a hiding place. At least nobody would be able to say that Annabel Mackinac had made her cry. She crouched under the branches and slumped down against the trunk of the tree.

The cool shade made her tears feel even hotter. She swiped at her cheeks. *I won't let her get to me*, she vowed. *I won't!*

"You should be out there getting back at her instead of hiding in here," a voice said.

Darcy flinched. "Who said that?"

Suddenly, a hand dropped down in front of Darcy's face. It was holding a bright red apple. "Hungry?"

Darcy shook her head. "No. . . ."

Then two feet in pointy black shoes and striped stockings dropped down. "Mind if I join you?" the voice said. A black shape floated down from a branch of the tree and landed on the soft pine needles.

Darcy gasped. It was a witch!

"Just thought I'd say hello to a fellow crone," the witch said. She grinned, and Darcy realized it was just a teenage girl in a cool outfit.

"That's a great costume," Darcy said politely. The girl had straggly hair and a long, pointed chin. She had an even bigger, uglier wart on her nose than Darcy did. The only thing that spoiled the effect was the pair of dark sunglasses perched on her long, skinny nose.

Darcy guessed her to be around sixteen or seventeen. A little old for costumes, but who could resist Halloween? And the high school kids loved to hang out at Wild Cody's grave.

"What's your name, kid?" the witch asked.

"Darcy Ryan," Darcy said. "What's yours?"

The girl didn't answer. She pointed a dirty, long fingernail at Darcy. "You shouldn't have let Golden Girl push you around," she said.

"I know," Darcy said. "But I didn't know what else to do."

"There's plenty to do if you know how," the witch said. She took a bite of her apple. "If you dress the part, you should act it. You could change her into a newt."

Darcy grinned, playing along. "That would be fun."

The girl pushed up her dark glasses. "You think so?" There was a little catch in her voice, as though she were pleased at Darcy's interest.

"Sure," Darcy said. "Annabel is a total Miss Priss. She used to live in L.A. Imagine what she'd do if she found herself changed into a tiny lizard! She'd gross herself out." Darcy giggled at the thought.

The girl tossed her apple core aside and reached into the folds of her black gown. "Let me see what I have. . . ."

She held up a vial. "Weasel bone, that won't help." She held up another small glass jar. "Ah-ha! Newt tongue. I think I might have enough!"

Darcy's grin wobbled. The girl seemed so serious! It was kind of scary.

The witch frowned as she slipped the vial back into her pocket. "I can't do it here, though. I need other ingredients. You'll have to come with me."

"That's nice of you. But I'm with my cousins," Darcy said politely. The girl was kidding, of course. But even if she wasn't, Darcy wasn't going anywhere with her. She seemed pretty weird.

The teenager didn't seem to hear her. "We'll go

back to my castle and prepare the potion. But first I have something to attend to here. I have to . . . wake someone up." She threw back her head and let loose a cackling laugh.

Darcy's polite smile froze on her lips. There was something about the laugh. . . . It chilled her right to the bone.

The girl tried to stand up, but almost hit her head on a branch. Bent over, she held out a bony hand to Darcy. "Come on, Darcy Ryan. Let me show you what to do with your enemies."

The girl's sunglasses slid down her nose, revealing her shining eyes.

Darcy gasped.

Her eyes were a deep, glowing red!

Darcy couldn't move. There was something there, something deep within the witch's gaze. It was . . . *evil*.